enemies

Svetlana Chmakova

enemies

SVETLANA CHMAKOVA

Coloring assistants: Effie Lealand, Melissa McCommon
Inking assistants: Effie Lealand, Young Kim
Lettering: JY Editorial

JY
150 West 30th Street, 19th Floor
New York, NY 10001

Visit us at jyforkids.com
facebook.com/jyforkids
twitter.com/jyforkids
jyforkids.tumblr.com
instagram.com/jyforkids

First JY Edition: September 2022

JY is an imprint of Yen Press, LLC.
The JY name and logo are trademarks of Yen Press, LLC.

The publisher is not responsible for websites (or their content) that are not owned by the publisher.

Library of Congress Control Number: 2022940170

ISBNs: 978-1-9753-1279-4 (hardcover)
978-1-9753-1272-5 (paperback)
978-1-9753-1278-7 (ebook)

1 3 5 7 9 10 8 6 4 2

LSC-C

Printed in the United States of America

Table of Contents

CHAPTER 1

MY NAME IS FELICITY TEALE.

SCRIBBLE SCRIBLE

ARTIST, WRITER, COSPLAYER, UNCONVINCED MIDDLE SCHOOLER.

SITTING HERE, PLOTTING AWESOME THINGS I'M GONNA DO.

AFTER I'M DONE WATCHING TV WITH THE FAM. (FOR **RESEARCH!**)

...YOU KNOW THAT SHOW PIRANHA PIT, WHERE PEOPLE PITCH THEIR BUSINESSES TO BIG-SHOT INVESTORS...

...TRYING TO GET A DEAL?

TAP TAP

— MARCELIO VARGA, TWELVE YEARS OLD, LOOKING FOR $100,000 FOR 40% OF HIS CAKE-DECORATING BUSINESS!

THEY GOT KIDS COMING ON A LOT, RUNNING THEIR OWN BUSINESSES LIKE IT'S NO BIG DEAL.

IMPRESSIVE SALES NUMBERS.

YOU HAVE SOME DECORATION SAMPLES?

HERE IS AN ANIME-THEMED CAKE DESIGN.

IT'S ONE OF OUR MOST POPULAR.

OHHHH!

HAPPY BDAY !!!

...!

WHAAAT? SERIOUSLY?! THAT?

...HMM?

HUH! THAT'S NOT A VERY GOOD DRAWING, IS IT.

NO IT'S NOT! PEOPLE PAY MONEY FOR THAT?

OOF, YOUR ART'S MUCH BETTER, BABY.

RIGHT?!

I COULD DRAW CIRCLES AROUND THIS KID!

MOM A.K.A. VIOLETTA

DAD A.K.A. ROBERT

...MAYBE PEOPLE PAY FOR IT BECAUSE IT'S ACTUALLY *DONE*. AND ON *TIME*. UNLIKE *YOUR* STUFF.

...

...I FINISH STUFF!

NO YOU DON'T.

"BABY" SISTER
A.K.A. LETTY

PFFT

NAME ONE THING I DIDN'T FINISH!

SURE.

THE ART CLUB POSTER.

...!

TH-THAT'S...

THAT WAS A *GROUP* PROJECT! *EVERYONE* WAS DROPPING THE BALL!

YOUR SAILOR SUNBURST COSTUME.

...OKAY, JUST BECAUSE DAD WANTED TO HELP—

NOOOO I DIDN'T.

7

OH, LET'S NOT FORGET YOUR BIKER ELVES WEBCOMIC.

....!

I DID...!

I DID TEN PAGES!!

BUT WAS IT *FINISHED*?

...

NO, IT WASN'T.

YOU JUST *STOPPED*.

YOUR THREE READERS WERE *CRYING* IN THE COMMENTS.

... *mumble*

I FINISHED...THE BIRTHDAY CARD...FOR YOUR UNGRATEFUL BUTT...

OH YES, IT WAS VERY NICE TO GET IT...

...ONE WEEK AFTER MY BIRTHDAY.

...

...CONGRATULATIONS, YOU HAVE A BITE!

OH, LOOK! THE ANIME-CAKE KID GOT FUNDING!

....!

...BECAUSE HE *FINISHES* STUFF.

TAP TAP

...

I COULD... FINISH STUFF...

RRING

MONDAY, SCHOOL DAY.

BERRYBROOK MIDDLE SCHOOL

STUPID LETTY.

SHE THINKS SHE'S SO COOL.

9

JUST BECAUSE SHE'S...

...ORGANIZED...

SLAM

...AND NEVER LATE...

...AND NEVER FORGETS STUFF...

...

...AND PLAYS THE PIANO, AND WINS AWARDS FOR HER SCIENCE STUFF, AND HAS A BANK ACCOUNT AT **TWELVE**...

...BUT WE ARE NOT GOING TO DWELL ON THAT.

IMPORTANT LIFE SURVIVAL TACTICS —

1. **DON'T** COMPARE YOURSELF TO OTHERS.
2. COMPARE YOURSELF TO THE **YOU** OF YESTERDAY.
3. WHAT WERE YOUR GOALS AND DREAMS?

4. GO GET 'EM.

SO THAT'S WHAT'S HAPPENING.

...RIGHT AFTER I MAKE IT TO CLASS ON TIME.

SCHOOL DAY AT BERRYBROOK MIDDLE — PRETTY TYPICAL.

TOO MANY CLASSES, TOO MUCH SCHOOLWORK.

RANDOM DRAMA IN THE HALLWAYS.

I SAW WHAT YOU POSTED ABOUT ME!!

WANNA SAY IT TO MY FACE?

um

n-no?...

uh

RANDOM DRAMA IN MY GROUP CHATS...

UGH

COME ON.

13

JOSEPH KOH

FRIENDSHIP STATUS:
COMPLICATED

WE USED TO BE FRIENDS IN ELEMENTARY SCHOOL.

THEN MIDDLE SCHOOL CAME...
I MADE MORE FRIENDS...

...AND HE DIDN'T.

I TRIED TO FIX THAT...

OH YEAH? OKAY!

HEY!

THIS IS MY FRIEND JOSEPH!

HE'S COOL, SO YOU SHOULD ALL LIKE HIM!

...BUT IT JUST MADE THINGS WEIRD.

...AND...

. . .

...THEY'RE STILL WEIRD.

UHHHH, GOTTA GO! MEETING ART CLUB PEEPS FOR LUNCH!

ALL RIGHT, LATER!

WE MOSTLY AVOID EACH OTHER NOW.

CAFETERIA

HAHA YAMMER

OMG, DID YOU SEE THE ANIME-CAKE-KID EPISODE YESTERDAY?!

YES!!

HOW DID HE GET FUNDING WITH THAT ART?!

UUGH. WOULD YOU TWO STOP TALKING ABOUT PIRANHA PIT?

RIGHT?!

...ANIME CAKE?

ART CLUB BUDDIES LUNCH TABLE

WE COULD DRAW BETTER CAKES WITH OUR FEET!

haha

FEET CAKE!

nooo.

TESS IS A PIRANHA PIT FAN TOO. WE GOT HOOKED WHEN...

hi grace.

HI.

do u want cookies?

uhh... maybe one box..

...WE HAD TO TEAM UP TO SELL GIRL SCOUT COOKIES AND NEEDED SALES TIPS.

WE SET UP AT THE LOCAL COMICS FESTIVAL ENTRANCE...

I'LL TAKE FIVE, PLS.

SOME FOR ME?

CAN I GET THREE?

...AND MADE BANK.

ARE YOU TALKING ABOUT *PIRANHA PIT* STUFF STILL?

LIKE ANY OF YOU COULD EVER RUN A BUSINESS.

YOU CAN'T EVEN FINISH A CLUB POSTER.

UGH.

KEEP WALKING, LETTY.

AKSHULLEEE...

...WE'RE EATING HERE TODAY.

SLIIIDE

....!

WHAT?! NO! WHY?!

ART CLUB AND SCIENCE CLUB ARE SUPPOSED TO BE FRIENDS NOW, REMEMBER?*

(*LOOOONG STORY)

LET'S BOND! DO YOU WANT TO HEAR ABOUT THAT STATE COMPETITION WE WON?

UGH. NO.

TOO BAD! SO, IT WAS THE LAST ROUND, AND—

WAIT— WHERE ARE YOU GOING?

ESCAPE

OH, UM!

I GOT LIBRARY BOOKS TO RETURN!

BYE.

LIBRARY

HI, FELICITY!

...hi, mrs pratt.

...

STUPID LETTY.

...YOU'RE AMAZING! A GENIUS! I **KNOW!**

YOU'RE THE PRIDE OF THE FAMILY, AND I'M...

...ME.

Sigh.

...PEOPLE ARE ALWAYS LIKE, "JUST BE YOURSELF! THE WORLD WILL CATCH ON."

BUT...IT'S LIKE...

...THE WORLD DIDN'T GET THE MEMO?

IT DOESN'T WANT YOU TO "JUST BE YOURSELF."

IT WANTS YOU TO IMPRESS.

TO WIN.

1000000?!..

RRRRING

...WHAT COULD I EVER WIN?

NEWSBOARD

MAYBE THERE'S AN ART CONTE—

...?

UH, UM, MRS. PRATT?

HMM?

BEEP BEEP

THAT, UH, "PITCH THE FUTURE" THING...

HOW DO PEOPLE ENTER THAT?

...AH, THE CONTEST?

THAT'S WITH THE ENTREPRENEUR CLUB.

THEY MEET HERE, EVERY FRIDAY.

DO YOU WANT TO REGISTER?

u-uh. okay...

RRING

FRIDAY.

LIBRARY

bu-bump bu-bump

...⇒*GULP*⇐

...

UH—

IS THIS THE... ENTREPRENEUR CLUB?

....?

YES!

HI!

ARE YOU A NEW MEMBER?

UHHH...

...SURE...?

WAVE

GREAT! COME ON OVER!

I AM MX. EDI, NEW LIBRARY TECH.

UHH...

FELICITY TEALE, STUDENT.

...IS THIS THE PLACE FOR THE "PITCH THE FUTURE" CONTEST?

IT SURE IS!!

WELCOME!

EEEEE

WE WERE JUST ABOUT TO START!

HERE'S THE CONTEST-INFO BOOKLET...

...AND THE WORKBOOK WE'RE USING.

GRAB A SEAT!

NOW, LET'S PICK UP WHERE WE LEFT OFF LAST WEEK!

SCRAPE

WE WENT OVER THE RULES, WE BRAINSTORMED IDEAS...

NOW LET'S TALK FORMAT!

THE FINAL PITCH OF YOUR IDEA NEEDS TO BE A VIDEO, SO—

SIT

GLANCE GLANCE

I BOOKED A VIDEO-EDITOR BUDDY OF MINE FOR A Q&A IN TWO WEEKS.

RRUSTLE

23

BLAH, BLAH, BUSINESS PLAN...

BLA BLA

...

JOSEPH? What are YOU doing here?!

ME?! What are YOU doing here?!

...

...AND MOST OF ALL, REMEMBER—THIS MAY BE A COMPETITION, BUT—

THE MAIN THING IS TO LEARN NEW STUFF AND HAVE FUN!

THAT WAY, *EVERYONE* WINS!

...

...EXCEPT *ACTUALLY* WINNING.

NOW, IS EVERYONE READY TO FORM THEIR TEAMS?

!

...YES, FELICITY? QUESTION?

UH... TEAMS...?

YES!

ONE OF THE JUDGMENT CRITERIA IS FOR COOPERATION AND TEAMWORK...

...SO YOU NEED TO HAVE AT LEAST ONE PARTNER.

...

YOU AND JOSEPH SEEM LIKE YOU KNOW EACH OTHER—

....!

DO YOU WANT TO BE A TEAM TOGETHER?

...

NO.

OH.

WOW.

INDUSTRIAL-STRENGTH AWKWARD AURAS...

I GUESS YOU WANT TO...

...FIND YOUR OWN PARTNERS?

...BY NEXT WEEK?

MONDAY.

RRING

A **PARTNER?**
ARGH!! PARTNERS
ARE A PAIN!

THEY MIGHT BE
MEAN, LIKE LETTY...

Y R U
STOOPID

...OR IRRESPONSIBLE, LIKE THAT GUY IN MY SPANISH CLASS.

CAN YOU AT LEAST DO SOME OF THE WORK?!

THIS IS A GROUP PROJECT!

NAW, YOU DO IT SO MUCH BETTER.

SLAM

...

UGH.

...I GOTTA PICK SOMEONE SAFE...

...SOMEONE WHO'LL DO THE WORK... WON'T BE A BUTT (TOO MUCH)...

HEH-HEH. I KNOW EXACTLY WHO.

RRING

...HEY, TESS.

WANNA JOIN A CLUB WITH ME?

HUH?

AND MAYBE WIN A THOUSAND DOLLARS?

GUH

WHA—?

27

AND BE COOL BOSS LADIES LIKE ON *PIRANHA PIT* AND START OUR OWN BUSINESS?

WHAAAA

OH HECK YEAH

FRIDAY.

HELLO!

THIS IS MY BUSINESS PARTNER, TESSA!

OH WOW, SO QUICK!

WELCOME, WELCOME!!

HAVE A SEAT!

HEE HEE HEE

TODAY'S TOPIC IS— BUSINESS PLANS! I GOT YOU SOME TEMPLATES TO HAND OUT...

So... is this our competition?

I think so.

Nice.

...

WHAT.

...OH HEY, 'CITY! YOU HERE TOO?!

NICE!

· · ·

UH.

HEY, ALEX.

and joseph

OH HEY!

Hiiiiiiiii!

I'M TESS! I'M FELICITY'S PARTNER!

'SUP, TESS, FELICITY'S PARTNER!

MAY THE BEST TEAM WIN, RIGHT?

TWIRL

· · ·

WINK

OH, WE PLAN TO.

HA HA

YEAH, LET'S GOOOOO.

r u... flirting ??

WHAT? PFFT. NO.

HIIIII, JOSEPH!

· · ·

HEE HEE

· · ·

HA HA HA

THIS...CAN ONLY END WELL...RIGHT?

CHAPTER 2

. . .

...EXHIBIT #100,000,000 WHY HAVING PARTNERS IS A BAD IDEA.

OH HEY, HOW'S THE PAGE GOING?

ARGH GO AWAY. LETTY.

...ALSO SIBLINGS. HAVING SIBLINGS IS A HORRIBLE IDEA.

RRWG

MONDAY.

SPANISH CLASS.

BERRYBROOK MIDDLE

¡CÁLMENSE POR FAVOR! HOY TRABAJAMOS EN SUS PROYECTOS GRUPALES.

...I MEAN, YOU KNOW HOW IT IS!

EVERY TIME THERE'S A MANDATORY GROUP PROJECT, YOU ALWAYS END UP WITH SOMEONE LIKE...

THIS KID.

...YOU DIDN'T DO ANY OF THE PREP?!

THIS IS A GROUP PRESENTATION!! DO YOUR PART!!

DENNIS THE DEADWEIGHT PARTNER

MNYEH MNYEH

YOU NAG LIKE MY MOM.

WE STILL GOT TIME. I'LL DO IT NEXT WEEK.

....!

IF YOU'RE SO WORRIED, JUST GIVE ME SOME LINES TO SAY, AND I'LL DO THAT.

I MEAN, WHAT DO YOU DO ABOUT **THAT**?!

...

GRRR

ok ...FINE.

sure.

PLAN PLAN

...HOW ABOUT THIS, FOR HIS RESTAURANT SCENE PART—

PLOT PLOT

SOY UN PLATO DE CACA. ¿DÓNDE ESTÁ EL BAÑO, POR FAVOR?

....!

ME GUSTA COMER MOCOS DEL FREGADERO.

HEH HEH HEH

THAT SOUND GOOD?

yes muy bueno.

YEAH, YEAH, WHATEVER.

HE DESERVES **EVERY WORD** OF THAT.

RRING

AT LEAST TESS IS *DEFFO* BETTER THAN THAT KID.

WE ROCKED THE GIRL SCOUT COOKIE SALES...WE'RE GOING TO *FLATTEN* THIS COMPETITION.

HEY, YO, 'CITY!

!

I SENT YOU SUPPLIES IN *SKORE*! DID YOU GET THEM?!

....!

NOT YET! WHAT ARE THEY?

WINK

H-HEY, JOSEPH.

...   ...

HA HA

CHECK IT AND FIND OUT!

AND DON'T FORGET, *SKORE* TOURNEY AT MY HOUSE THIS WEEKEND!

OH, I'LL BE THERE!

TO KICK YOUR BUTT!!

ha ha

YOU WISH! LATER.

LATER!

...

...

...YEP. THINGS ARE STILL WEIRD.

HE PROBABLY DOESN'T WANT ME TO BE THERE...

WELL, WHATEVER.

HA HA

SKORE IS LIKE, MY **ONE** JOY IN LIFE RIGHT NOW.

AND ALEX KEEPS INVITING ME, SOOO...

checking SKORE

...WHAT DID HE SEND ME THIS TIME...

BATTALEX

sent you a gift

PLASMA CHARGES (3)

ACCEPT

NO THANX

DECIDE LATER

ALEX'S SKORE AVATAR

OOH, I NEEDED THOSE!

accept

...JOSEPH'S NEVER EVEN MESSAGED ME IN-GAME...

...NEVER MIND GIFTS.

RRING

LUNCH.

FELICITY, OVER HERE!!

READY TO BRAINSTORM TOTAL CONTEST DOMINATION?!!

YEEAAAH

GONNA CRUSH THIS LIKE WE DID THE GIRL SCOUT COOKIE SALES!!

YEAAAH!

BOSS LADIES!

...OKAY, SO, STEP ONE— COME UP WITH AN AWESOME IDEA...

OOOOH! I GOT TONS!

RRUSTLE

...THAT FOLLOWS THE RULES.

...

oh yeah.

the rules.

what r they?

"CREATE A BUSINESS PROPOSAL THAT FILLS A NEED OR SOLVES A PROBLEM FOR PEOPLE AND SOCIETY."

hmmm

FILLS... A NEED...

...EVERYONE... NEEDS... FOOD... AND... CLOTHES...?

...OH!!

I KNOW!

A CAFÉ/ BOUTIQUE!!

...HMM...

WHAT?! IT'S PERFECT! IT FILLS TWO NEEDS!

IN, LIKE, A WAAAY BOUGIE WAY, THOUGH.

...ALSO, THERE'S KIND OF ALREADY A LOT OF CAFÉS AND BOUTIQUES...

IT'S NOT TOO ORIGINAL.

....!

...W-WELL, THERE'S NOT THAT MANY CAFÉ **AND** BOUTIQUES...

41

...

UH, OKAY... HOW ABOUT THIS—

YOU KNOW HOW SOME PEOPLE SMELL?

WE COULD START A SCENTED PRODUCT LINE—LIKE CANDLES, SOAPS, DEODORANTS, AND HAND OUT BASKETS TO PEOPLE, HA-HA!

BIG SERVICE TO SOCIETY!

THAT'S KINDA...MEAN.

YOU DON'T KNOW WHAT THEY GOT GOING ON.

...!

...ALSO, EVERYONE AND THEIR *CAT* MAKES CANDLES AND SOAPS.

OUR NEIGHBOR MAKES THEM FOR HER ONLINE STORE. THEY **SMELL**.

...

WELL, WHAT ARE *YOUR* IDEAS?

HMMMM

HOW ABOUT...

...HELPING PEOPLE GET GROCERIES HOME?

...ISN'T THERE AN APP FOR THAT?

UH...ONLINE TUTORING!

DEFINITELY APPS FOR THAT. ALSO, SCHOOL DOES THIS.

...HELPING OLD PEOPLE USE TECH?

MY GRANDMA HAS A TIKTOK. THEY'RE **FINE**.

...THIS IS *HARD!*

YEAH. NO KIDDING!

I GUESS THAT'S WHY THE PRIZE IS A THOUSAND DOLLARS.

HMMM

RRRING

NEXT DAY.

...OKAY, SLIGHT SETBACK. GOOD IDEAS = NOT AS EASY AS THEY SEEM...

HMM...SOLVES A NEED...HELPS SOCIETY...AND IS NOT, LIKE...

...STUPID HARD FOR MIDDLE GRADERS TO DO...MAYBE I SHOULD ASK MOM AND DAD FOR HELP?

...NO! LETTY NEVER ASKS THEM FOR HELP. I'LL, UH...I'LL CHECK THE LIBRARY!

LUNCH.

LIBRARY

...WHAT SHOULD I EVEN LOOK FOR? UGH...IDEA, IDEA...

....!

...JOSEPH.

SCAN SCAN

MU N CH

HE LOOKING TO GET IN TROUBLE OR SOMETHING?

SNORT

TYPE TYPE

...WHO'S HE TYPING TO—

!

uh

...**NOT** SUPPOSED TO HAVE FOOD IN THE LIBRARY, HELLO?

TEN OVERDUE BOOKS ON THE WALL, TEN OVERDUE BOOKS!

....!

IF ONE OF THESE BOOKS SHOULD HAPPEN TO BE RETURNED...

uh uh

TYPE TYPE

um

u-uh HI MX.EDI!!

OH! HI, FELICITY!

CAN I HELP YOU?

UH, YEAH, MX.EDI, UM I'M WONDERING ABOUT—

SHIELD

HA-HA, NO NEED TO YELL. I'M RIGHT HERE!

OH, HAHA. YEAH I'M JUST...

escape escape

UH... EXCITED? ABOUT THE CONTEST

PHEW

OH, THAT'S SO GREAT TO HEAR!

YOU AND TESSA MUST BE ALREADY SETTLED ON AN IDEA!

...!

O-OH, UH, WE'RE ACTUALLY HAVING TROUBLE COMING UP WITH ONE...

I'M LOOKING FOR SOME...BOOKS OR SOMETHING? FOR HELP.

OH! I JUST FINISHED A DISPLAY! FOR THAT!

COME SEE!

MAKE SOAP!

KID BIZ BIG IDEAS (it's soap)

HO ST

SOAP! SOAP! SOAP! &CANDLES

SENIOR TECH SUPPORT

BU FO ID

GRAB ANYTHING YOU LIKE!

... ...uh

45

WE NEED TO STEP UP OUR *GAME* IF WE'RE GONNA *COMPETE* AND BE CHANGE-MAKERS!

THERE ARE KIDS OUT THERE SOLVING *POVERTY! HUNGER!* INVENTING THE *FUTURE!*

I GOT THESE BOOKS FOR US, AND I HAVE A WHOLE BUNCH OF LINKS—

...OOH, ARTISAN SOAP!

NO SOAP!! AND NO CANDLES!!

START a kid bi how-t idea

HEY.

EVERYONE NEEDS SOAP. IT'S *GOOD* HYGIENE!!

IT'S NECESSARY IN OUR SOCIETY! IT PREVENTS DISEASES!

LET'S DO LITERALLY ANYTHING ELSE...!

AH! TOTE BAGS! WE COULD PUT COOL SLOGANS...

TOTE BAGS... ARE NOT... A NEED...

SAYS *YOU.*

I ALWAYS NEED CUTE TOTE BAGS...

TIC
TOC
TIC
TOC

HALF AN HOUR LATER.

UUUGHH~!!

WHY R U BEING SO DIFFICULT!!

...

UGH, WHATEVER, I GOTTA GO. I HAVE CHOIR PRACTICE.

CALL ME WHEN YOU HAVE YOUR BRILLIANT IDEA.

see ya

BYE.

...

HWOOo~

NEXT DAY.

SLAM

RRRNNG

...

NOTHING!

...WELL, I GOT IDEAS, BUT THEY'RE JUST OKAY...

HOW DO PEOPLE COME UP WITH THE WINNER IDEAS?!

...HOW DOES LETTY DO IT?

I SAW YOUR IDEA ON THE PROJECT BOARD!! IT'S *BRILLIANT*!!

YEAH, MISS TOBINS LIKED IT TOO!

SHE SAID IT'S FIRST PLACE MATERIAL!

SHE MAKES IT LOOK SO EASY...

HEY, 'CITY! 'SUP!!

DO YOU ALL HAVE YOUR IDEA YET?

...!

H-HEY, ALEX. U-UH...

GUESS WHAT— WE ALREADY GOT OURS!!

WHAT?!

ALREADY?!

YEAH!! YOU WANNA HEAR IT?

UH, S-SU—

HEY, WHA? NO...!

...HUH?

WE'RE NOT SUPPOSED TO SHARE!

THIS IS A *CONTEST*!

awkward aura

...OH.

UH, LATER!

...SKORE TOURNEY, SATURDAY, MY PLACE! DON'T FORGET!

YEAH, YEAH! I'LL BE THERE!

...WELL, WHATEVS. HAVE TO GO ANYWAY.

SEE YOU LATER.

. . .

...YEP. AWKWARD DISASTER CENTRAL.

CALLED IT.

ugh

...COME ONNN, IDEA, IDEA, IDEA...

FRIDAY.

OKAY, EVERYONE, LET'S SETTLE DOWN!

YAMMER

HEY!

HA HA

CLUB MEETING IS STARTING!

...HEY.

. . .

hey.

...DID YOU EVER COME UP WITH AN IDE—

GUH!

NO...

uh.

ARE YOU OKAY?!!

HAVE YOU SLEPT?!

not sure...?

i watched... so many videos... and read... so many articles...

BUT *NOTHING*.

ALL THESE KIDS OUT THERE DOING AMAZING STUFF.

WHY CAN'T WE COME UP WITH GOOD IDEAS...?

HEY, *MY* IDEAS ARE GOOD!

COME *ONNN*, SOAPS AND TOTE BAGS AREN'T GONNA WIN US THIS COMPETITION.

YOU CAN'T KNOW FOR SURE UNLESS YOU TRY!

NO ONE EVER WON WITH THAT!!

POP!

DID I JUST DETECT *STRESS* ABOUT WINNING? INSTEAD OF LEARNING AND HAVING FUN?!

COME ON, YOU TWO! THIS PROJECT IS NOT ABOUT WINNING! IT'S ABOUT WORKING TOGETHER!

YES, MX. EDI.

YOU SURE DID.

. . .

TRYING THINGS! LEARNING NEW STUFF!

GAINING NEW SKILLS!

YEAH, YEAH! THAT'S RIGHT!

MY ROOMIE JUST GOT THIS STRAWBERRY-VANILLA SCENT AND—

MX. EDI, DON'T *YOU* THINK SOAP'S A GREAT IDEA?

OMG *YES, I LOVE IT!!* WHAT KIND WILL YOU MAKE?!

. . .

SLUMP

nnngh

I JUST REALLY WANT TO WIN THIS.

WHY DOESN'T ANYONE UNDERSTAND...

YOOOO

KTK

JOSEPH, ALEX! YOU MADE IT! AGAIN!

MX. EDI, WE HAVE OUR IDEA!!

CAN WE PITCH?!

NOT YET! YOU NEED TO FILL OUT THE BUSINESS PLAN TEMPLATE!

...

...UH.

OH YEAH.

....!

...

...

...

Hiiii, ALEX
Hiii, JOSEPH

SO THEN, BUSINESS PLANS—

YO!

THIS ALL **SUCKS**.

HOW DO THEY WORK?!!

LET'S TALK ABOUT ALL THE—

UGH, I WISH I HADN'T AGREED TO ALEX'S TOURNEY TOMORROW.

WHAT D'YOU WANNA BET IT'S GONNA BE EXTRA AWKWARD AND ZERO FUN?!

CHAPTER 3

57

SH-K-T-

WINNER: nNilayTion!

NOOOO!!

YESSS

MY TURN, MY TURN!!

AVENGE ME, 'CITY.

PLOP

NILAY, LOVE THAT NEW SHOULDER CANNON.

thanx

...I THINK I'LL **TAKE** IT!

DO IT!

TAKE HIS SONIC DAGGER TOO!

I LOVE PLAYING WITH THESE IDIOTS.

OH, YOU CAN TRY. YOU CAN—

—WOAH HEY!!

GET 'IM 'CITY!!

OMG, NILAY, YOUR POI—

YOU GOT THE RED THUNDER BUGS?! WHEN?!

heh heh heh

SKORE IS FUN, BUT...

...EVEN TIC-TAC-TOE WOULD BE, WITH THIS CREW.

(EXTRA FUN, SINCE JOSEPH DIDN'T SHOW UP, I GUESS.)

WHOA, TRIPLE COMBO!

nice

ARGH!

NILAY, YOUR SHIELD!!

SHOULDER CANNON = GET!

DING DONG

ALEX!

JOSEPH IS HERE. COME GREET YOUR FRIEND!

JO, FINALLY!! C'MON, GET IN HERE!

...

YOU ALMOST MISSED IT!!

WE'RE DOING LIGHTNING ROUNDS— 'CITY'S ABOUT TO WIPE THE FLOOR WITH NILAY!

'CITY, WATCH OUT!!

SHKT

-2,000

+5,000

SHKT

...GUH!!

DUDE, WHAT ARE YOU DOING?! PUT UP YOUR SHIELDS!!

-5000

CITYSCRAPE
-10000

-8HP

nNilayTion WINS.

WINNING STREAK!

UNDEFEATED CHAMPION!!

YEEEAH!

ARGH!!

'CITY, NOOO! YOU HAD HIM ON THE ROPES. WHAT DID YOU DOOOOOO!

THE...THE DOORBELL THREW ME OFF!

...!

ARE YOU BLAMING ME FOR LOSING?

...N-NO!

I SAID THE DOORBELL.

UH, C-COME ON, WE'RE ALL FRIENDS HERE, RIGHT?

...

...

...RIGHT...?

ALEX, PIZZA IS HERE! FEED YOUR FRIENDS!

oh good.

...

WAIT, WHAT?!

YOU'RE STARTING A BUSINESS?!

YEP! FOR A BIZ COMPETITION!

GRAND PRIZE IS A THOUSAND DOLLARS.

A THOUSAND BUCKS?! *NICE!*

I WANNA WIN THAT!

YEAH, YOU AND LIKE SIX HUNDRED OTHER PEOPLE. haha

YOU GOTTA FIGHT FOR IT!

...

GET A *REAL WINNER* IDEA!

HA HA

OH WHAT, YOUR LOSER BUTT'S GOT ONE?

YEEPPP.

WE HAVE THE *BEST* IDEA. IT'S LIKE PRINTING MONEY.

SEROUS?! WHAT IS IT?

WAIT!

OKAY, SO, WE'RE GONNA—

COME ON, YOU CAN'T JUST TELL IT TO EVERYONE!

AW!

WHY NOT?!

...WE HAVE AN ENEMY SPY IN OUR MIDST.

....?

...ENEMY?

WHAAAT?

'CITY'S NOT A SPY!!

I'M JUST *SAYING*.

SHE'S IN THE COMPETITION TOO...

SO WHAT...?! IT'S NOT LIKE SHE'LL STEAL OUR IDEA OR WHATEVER.

FELICITY'S GOOD PEOPLE.

...

...THAT'S RIGHT! THIS IS DUMB...

SEE YOU MONDAY, ALEX!

LATER!

...FELICITY, YOU NEED A RIDE HOME?

UH, NO, MY DAD'S ON HIS WAY! I'M GONNA WAIT OUTSIDE.

PHEW.

MAYBE I SHOULD START AVOIDING JOSEPH HERE TOO—

...FELICITY?

UHHH.

JOSEPH'S MOM

H-HELLO, MRS. KOH.

IT'S SO NICE TO SEE YOU! IT'S BEEN SO LONG!

WE MISS YOUR VISITS... BUT JOSEPH TOLD US HOW BUSY YOU ARE WITH SCHOOL.

...

o-oh yes. so busy.

WELL, I LOOK FORWARD TO SEEING YOU AT THE PARTY.

uh... party?

...

JOSEPH'S BIRTHDAY PARTY! YOU ALL HAD SUCH FUN WITH A GAME THEME LAST YEAR— WE'RE THINKING OF DOING IT AGAIN!

JOSEPH, DIDN'T YOU ALREADY GIVE THE INVITE?

u-uh.

...

...

n-no not yet.

WELL, DON'T FORGET! I'M GOING TO DROP THIS FOOD OFF.

AND BE RIGHT OUT!

...

HONK

OH, THAT'S MY DAD!

BYEEE!

SLAM

HI, BABY, HOW'D YOU DO?

DID YOU KICK BUTT?

...

...DAD, HAS ANYONE EVER CALLED YOU THEIR "ENEMY"?

HA HA

YOUR MOM, EVERY TIME I FINISH THE LAST OF HER ICE CREAM.

I-I MEAN...IS THAT THE RIGHT USE?! FOR THAT WORD?

NAW, SHE'S JUST KIDDING.

I MEAN, IT'S JUST ICE CREAM—I GO AND GET HER ANOTHER TUB. OR TWO.

heh heh

...NOW, WHO'S OUT THERE CALLING *YOU* ENEMY?

WHO DO I *DESTROY*?

O-OH, JUST THIS KID I KNOW.

I DON'T KNOW IF HE WAS KIDDING.

WELL... IS HE *YOUR* ENEMY?

...

I...DON'T KNOW?

...

IT'S ALL... WEIRD.

WELL, JOKE OR NOT, IF YOU'RE NOT OKAY WITH IT, HE BETTER STOP.

NOW BUCKLE IN, WE GOTTA GO PICK UP LETTY.

UUUGH

RRRING

BERRYBROOK MIDDLE

search search

Enemy *noun.*
1. One who is antagonistic to another.

...

HMMM

KTK

You're invited!

JOSEPH'S BIRTHDAY PARTY!

OH, JO'S INVITE.

MATH.

covert search

SIGH

CAFETER

PREEN PREEN

AND MISS TOBINS LOVED IT. SHE EVEN SAID—

CONTEST... *AWARDS*... *WIN*...

...

SIIIGH

...!

...!

HEY.

HEY.

SOOOO...

DID YOU COME UP WITH YOUR BRILLIANT IDEA?

UUUGH

I'LL TAKE THAT AS A "NO."

LIKE, I GOT PLENTY OF IDEAS, BUT...

OKAY, LET ME SEE.

FLIP FLIP

....!

PLASTIC... RECYCLED INTO PAVING STONES... *THAT'S COOL...* ...RESCUE-CAT CAFÉ?!

...WOW, AN ORGANIZER SITE FOR MEAL TRAINS?! MY MOM WOULD *KILL* FOR AN APP LIKE THAT!

...

...HEY, THESE IDEAS ARE REALLY GOOD!

WHY DON'T YOU LIKE THESE?!

BECAUSE SOMEONE ALREADY DID THEM!!

HUH...?

EVERY TIME...

...I'D COME UP WITH AN IDEA...I'D SEARCH IT AND FIND SOMEONE DOING THAT EXACT THING!! *ugh.*

WOW, REALLY?!

ALL OF THESE?

NO *WAY...*

search search

REALLY?

TAP TAP

HUH, WOW.

I GUESS PEOPLE HAVE BEEN BUSY DOING ALL THE THINGS...

YEP

PLOP

...

WELL, WE GOTTA COME UP WITH **SOMETHING** ANYWAY!

WE CAN'T **QUIT**!

WE CRUSHED COOKIE SALES! WE'RE FUTURE BOSS LADIES!

...OH YEAH, APPARENTLY, SAYING "BOSS LADIES" ISN'T COOL ANYMORE.

WHAT?

SAYS WHO?

INTERNET...

ARGH!!

WHO DECIDES THESE THINGS?!

STUPID INTERNET!

...

WELL, WE STILL CAN'T QUIT.

I ALREADY TOLD MY MOM I'M DOING THIS.

LET'S **DO IT.** LET'S MAKE THIS **WORK.**

YEAH. OKAY.

BOSS LADIES.

GLAD I HAVEN'T TOLD...

...MY PARENTS...

TEALE RESIDENCE.

FAMILY DINNER NIGHT.

SIZZLE SIZZLE

LETTY!

YOU CAN START SETTING THE TABLE!

OKAY!

CHOP CHOP

...

CHOP CHO

YOU OKAY, BABY? YOU BEEN QUIET LATELY.

O-OH, YEAH, YEAH! FINE!

JUST...THINKING.

EYE

HMM

...

I WAS JUST TALKING WITH MRS. KOH TODAY...

...O-OH, YEAH?

...AND REALIZED HOW LONG IT'S BEEN SINCE JOSEPH'S BEEN OVER HERE.

YOU TWO USED TO BE TIGHT!

EVERYTHING OKAY?

...W-WHO? OH YEAH, YEAH!

WE'RE JUST... REALLY BUSY...

I MEAN, SCHOOL'S A LOT, Y'KNOW?

OOF, YEAH!

NO *KIDDING.*

. . .

THEY REALLY LOAD YOU KIDS UP, THESE DAYS.

ALL THOSE NEW SUBJECTS...

Y-YEAH.

IT'S *HARD!*

IT'S NOT *THAT* HARD! YOU JUST NEED TO USE YOUR *BRAIN!*

IF YOU HAD ONE.

PFFT!

ha ha ha ha

. . .!

GASP!

LETTY!!

BABY, WHAT A MEAN THING TO SAY TO YOUR SISTER!

. . .!

S-SORRY.

. . .

DON'T SAY SORRY TO ME. APOLOGIZE TO HER!

. . .

s-sorry...

WHATEVER.

STALK STALK

73

MAYBE DR. LETTY TEALE, PhD. ONE DAY, HMM?

GET SOME OF THOSE SMART COOKIE SCHOLARSHIPS?

THAT'S THE PLAN!

AND WHAT ABOUT YOU, JELLY BEAN?

....!

STILL DRAWING THAT BIG-EYE ANIMU STUFF?

UH—

C'MON, MA. IT'S *ANIME*. HOW MANY TIMES I GOTTA SAY IT?

WELL, IT'S HARD TO REMEMBER ALL THAT SILLY STUFF.

UM.

IT'S NOT SILLY! THERE ARE REAL JOBS FOR THAT OUT THERE!

DRAWING SILLY CARTOONS? THAT'S NOT A REAL JOB.

MA, I SWEAR!

I'M JUST WORRIED FOR MY FUTURE!

...

...

I AM STARTING A BUSINESS WITH A FRIEND!

chew
chew

...

REALLY? I HAVEN'T HEARD ABOUT THIS! SOUNDS EXCITING.

Y-YEAH, IT'S... IT'S FOR THIS CONTEST...

THE GRAND PRIZE IS A THOUSAND DOLLARS.

FOR REAL? THAT'S A GOOD CHUNK OF CHANGE!

WELL, I'M NOT SURPRISED—YOU KNOW THE BUSINESS GENE RUNS IN THE FAMILY!

YOUR COUSIN TREY, HE OWNS THAT BAKERY BIZ!

AND MARISSA. SHE DID THAT—

...   ...

SHHH

VMMMM

...

VMM

UGH, WHY DID I TELL EVERYONE ABOUT THAT?!

NOW I CAN'T SECRETLY QUIT...

VMMMM

RRRING

BERRYBROOK MIDDLE SCHOOL

FRIDAY.

WELCOME BACK, EVERYONE!

I HOPE YOU ALL HAD A GOOD WEEK...

...AND HAVE YOUR BUSINESS IDEAS ALL DECIDED!

THE CONTEST *DEADLINE* IS APPROACHING!

TODAY, WE'RE GOING TO START PRACTICING YOUR *PITCHES!*

YOU CAN SHARE YOUR IDEA...

...AND GET USEFUL FEEDBACK!

SOOOOO... WHO WANTS TO GO FIRST?

....!

W-WAIT

GASP!

UH

OMG YES!! FINALLY

OOH, ALEX AND JOSEPH, ALL RIGHT!

SO, TO WARM UP, TELL US WHAT MADE YOU THINK OF YOUR BUSINESS...

...AND THEN WHAT YOUR IDEA IS.

YOU GOT IT, MX. EDI!

...

SO, UH, MY LITTLE BRO WAS IN THE HOSPITAL FOR LIKE TWO MONTHS AND IT WAS ROUGH ON HIM, Y'KNOW? IT SUCKED.

AND HE LOVES SKORE, HAS HIS OWN AVATAR AND ALL, SO...

...TO CHEER HIM UP, JO, HE—

JO, TELL THEM WHAT YOU CAME UP WITH!

....!

O-OH, UH... ONE OF THOSE...

PHOTOPRINTING SITES? LIKE...

AN IMAGE... BLANKET...

PRINT?

...WE MADE CAM A PERSONALIZED *SKORE* BLANKET WITH CAM'S AVATAR AND NAME!!!

SKORE

Y-YEAH, THAT.

IT WAS SO COOL!! ALL THE OTHER KIDS ON CAM'S FLOOR WANTED ONE!

SO THAT'S OUR IDEA— PERSONALIZED *SKORE* MERCH FOR SICK KIDS AND WHOEVER ELSE WANTS IT!

WOW.

....!

...WOW.

I WANT ONE.

COOL.

THAT BLANKET IS AWESOME.

..!

...WOW.

THAT'S... BRILLIANT.

BUT...

WAIT...

...HOW DID YOU GET PERMISSION TO PRINT ART FROM *SKORE*?

HUH?

THE WHAT?

PERMISSION...

...FOR THE...

IT'S ALL COPYRIGHTED STUFF IN *SKORE*?

THE ART...

W-WE DON'T NEED TO. IT'S ALL ONLINE, SO IT'S FREE TO USE. IT'S *PUBLIC DOMAIN*.

...!

UH, P-PRETTY SURE THAT'S...NOT...

MY ART'S ONLINE! AND IT'S *NOT* UP FOR GRABS.

POP!

UH, I THINK IT IS...

SO, HEY! FELICITY BRINGS UP AN EXCELLENT POINT!

WHEN SOMETHING IS POSTED ONLINE, IT DOES *NOT* MEAN IT'S FREE TO USE!

THERE ARE COPYRIGHT LAWS ABOUT THIS...

IF YOU SEE AN IMAGE YOU WANT TO USE—YOU NEED TO GET PERMISSION FROM THE CREATOR!

I CAN HELP YOU DRAFT THE REQUEST LETTER TO *SKORE*!

ONCE YOU GET THAT SORTED OUT...

...YOU'VE GOT AN AMAZING BUSINESS IDEA!

...HUH!

OKAY.

WE'LL DO THAT, THEN.

THIS WAS A GREAT PITCH! ROUND OF APPLAUSE, YOU ALL!

CLAP

...

CLAP

CLAP

CLAP

...

NOW, WHO WANTS TO PITCH THEIR IDEA NEXT?!

RASHID AND STEPHANOS— YOURS WAS REALLY EXCITING TOO. DO YOU WANT TO GO NEXT?

...UH.

OKAY.

...

SCRAPE

...

TIC

TOC

TIC

TOC

OOPS, LOOKS LIKE WE'LL HAVE TO FINISH THE PITCHES NEXT WEEK!

GREAT WORK, EVERYONE!

DON'T FORGET TO GET ME YOUR PERMISSION FORMS FOR OUR CLUB FIELD TRIP ON WEDNESDAY.

LIBRARY

OKAY, SO UH...

...WAS IT JUST ME, OR WERE MOST OF THOSE IDEAS KINDA...NOT GOOD?

YOU'RE TOO NICE—THEY *SUCKED*.

OURS ARE SO MUCH BETTER!! WE CAN *GET* IT!

I MEAN, *RIGHT*?! I'M EXCITED AGAIN!

WE STILL GOTTA SETTLE ON AN IDEA, THOUGH.

WE'LL DO IT THIS WEEK! AND PRESENT ON FRIDAY!

YEAAH!!

...YOU LOOK HAPPY.

....!

H-HEY, JOSEPH.

I-IS THAT YOUR PLAN? TO WIN?

MAKE UP PROBLEMS FOR OTHER PEOPLE'S PROJECTS?

W-WHA...?

I DIDN'T MAKE IT UP!

MX. EDI...

THEY SAID IT'S A PROBLEM TOO!

CHAPTER 4

RRRING

MONDAY.

BERRYBROOK MIDDLE

SOOOO.

WHAT'S THE DEAL WITH YOU AND THAT JOSEPH KID?

...!

YOU TWO GET ALL WEIRD AROUND EACH OTHER.

UGH, I DON'T EVEN KNOW!

...DOES HE HAVE A CRUSH ON YOU?

...NAW.

HE'D BE NICE TO A GIRL HE LIKES. HE'S NOT DUMB.

...HE HAD A GIRLFRIEND IN ELEMENTARY SCHOOL FOR, LIKE, FIVE SECONDS, AND HE GAVE HER ALL HIS COOKIES.

IT WAS SO CUTE.

WHAT.

ARGH!

WHO WAS IT?!

UHHH...OLESYA...? WE WERE ALL, LIKE, NINE...

SHE HAD TO LEAVE. HER PARENTS MOVED TO, LIKE, **THE ARCTIC CIRCLE** OR SOMETHING.

GLOOOOM

HE WAS **NOT** OKAY.

I DREW HIM CARTOONS FOR **WEEKS** TO CHEER HIM UP.

SO, WAIT, YOU WERE FRIENDS?

YEP.

...BUT OBVIOUSLY NOT ANYMORE.

WOW. WHAT *HAPPENED?*

I DON'T KNOW!

ARGH!

RRRING

WHOOP, GONNA BE LATE FOR SPANISH!

DASH DASH

HISTORY, FOR ME! SEE YOU AT LUNCH!

OKAY!

SPANISH.

OKAY, OKAY.

¡CÁLMENSE POR FAVOR!

HA HA

Yammer chatter

HOY VOLVEREMOS A TRABAJAR EN PRESENTACIONES GRUPALES.

MORE GROUP PROJECT WORK TODAY!

YAWN

UUUGH.

WAKE ME UP WHEN YOU'RE DONE.

DENNIS

AGAIN.

WHAT?! NO! DO SOME WORK!!

nope.

...

...OKAY, FINE, WHATEVER.

THE WHOLE CLASS WILL LAUGH AT YOU WHEN WE PRESENT...

...AND YOU'LL DESERVE IT.

¡HOLA! DENNIS, FELICITY, JAIME, HOW ARE YOU?

I AM CHECKING EVERYONE'S GROUP WORK TODAY.

u-uh.

LET'S SEE...

YES, YES, THIS IS VERY GOOD.

FUN THEME, GREAT SENTENCE CONSTRUCTION, GOOD VOCABULARY...

...DENNIS, YOU ARE QUITE THE COMEDIAN, I SEE!

HUH?

YOUR LINES!

YOU SAY HERE THAT YOU ARE A PLATE OF POOP?

ha ha

WHAT?!

....!

HA-HA, THIS IS GOLD! "I AM A PLATE OF POOP! WHERE IS THE BATHROOM? I LIKE TO EAT MY FOOD FROM A SINK!"

IT'S A BOLD JOKE, YES?

....

CAFETERIA

RING

SLAM

SLIDE

OKAY, WHO WANTS TO FIGHT ME?!

YOU'LL BE SORRY!

HA-HA, WHAT.

I'LL FIGHT YOU, BUT YOU HAVE TO PAY ME.

...DENNIS FOUND OUT WHAT HIS SPANISH LINES MEAN, FINALLY.

OMG! WHAT DID HE DOOOO?

THREW A BIG BABY TANTRUM!

SAID "U'LL PAY TEALE"

HE'S PROBABLY MAKING REVENGE PLANS RIGHT NOW—

WITH THE BIGGEST CRAYON HE CAN FIND.

HA HA HA

HEY, ART NERDS.

WHAT'S SO FUNNY?

UGH YOUR *FACE!*

WHAT ARE YOU DOING HERE?

OH, JUST ON THE WAY TO OUR TABLE, GONNA TALK **STRATEGY** TO GET FIRST PLACE AT THE...

...STATE STEM FAIR... _AGAIN_.

THAT'S CUTE.

IS _YOUR_ PRIZE A THOUSAND DOLLARS?

HUH?

UH... NO.

BECAUSE OURS IS. RIGHT, TESS?

YEP.

HUH?

WHAT PRIZE?

OH, IT'S A BIZ COMPETITION, YOU WOULDN'T KNOW ABOUT IT.

...OH, THE ENTREPRENEUR CLUB THING!

....

IS THAT THE ONE YOU WERE TALKING ABOUT?

....!!

uh
y-yes?

wait.
whaaat.

...ARE YOU TELLING EVERYONE ABOUT MY COMPETITION?

...!

IT'S NOT... *YOUR* COMPETITION!

M-MAYBE OTHERS WANT TO DO IT TOO!

...*OTHERS*?!

LIKE *WHO*?

...WAAAIT.

ARE *YOU* ENTERING?

...!

JUST TO SHOW OFF HOW MUCH BETTER YOU ARE?

UUGH.

GROW UP! YOU DON'T *OWN* THAT COMPETITION!

YOU'RE SUCH A CHILD.

YOU'RE THE CHILD!

I'M OLDER!

WELL, YOU SHOULD ACT LIKE IT!

MAKE ME!

BLEEAH

BLEEAH

WEDNESDAY, ENTREPRENEUR CLUB FIELD TRIP.

OKAY, WHO'S READY FOR THISSSS?!

THE SHELF

BOOKSTORE

I AM!! YESSSS, THE SHELF, I LOVE THIS STORE!

...

look look

...ARE YOU STILL FREAKING OUT ABOUT YOUR SISTER?

RELAX, IF SHE WAS JOINING, SHE'D BE HERE! NO WAY SHE'D MISS THIS!

...

THAT'S TRUE...

I GUESS I WORRIED OVER NOTHING.

THERE'S NO PROBLEM, RIGHT...?

...

SIDE EYE

...

...WELL, EXCEPT THIS.

HELLOOO!

BERRYBROOK FIELD TRIP CREW IS HERE!

HELLO, HELLO! WELCOME!

FSSS

SLIDE

BOOKS ♥

OH WOW, BIG CLUB! YOU ALL GONNA BE ENTREPRENEURS, HUH?

I'M SHEP.

AND I'M MARIA ROSALYN DÍAZ!

MX. SHEPARD AND MS. DÍAZ HAVE KINDLY AGREED TO SHARE SOME DETAILS ABOUT WHAT'S INVOLVED IN RUNNING A BUSINESS!

THEY WILL ALSO ANSWER SOME QUESTIONS, SO HAVE YOURS READY!

HOW MUCH MONEY DO YOU MA—

...AT THE END!! PLEASE WAIT UNTIL THE END!

97

OKAY, SHOW OF HANDS, WHO HASN'T BEEN IN OUR STORE BEFORE? ...A FEW OF YOU, OKAY—

OHHH, LOOK, TWO NEW ONES ON THE AUTOGRAPH WALL!

INA CRUZ AND J.Y. SMITH?!

NICE!

TESSA, FELICITY! PLEASE STAY WITH THE GROUP FOR THE TOUR.

BLAH BLAH

BLAH BLAH

OOPS, SORRY MX. EDI!

I DON'T NEED A TOUR.

DAD'S BEEN TAKING ME AND LETTY HERE SINCE WE WERE IN DIAPERS.

THERE'S THEIR HUGE MANGA SECTION...

*...AND THERE'S THE COFFEE/SNACK BAR. (THE FUDGE BROWNIES ARE THE **BEST**.)*

THEY ALSO GOT THIS "READING CORNER" FOR AUTHOR VISITS AND THEIR LOCAL BOOK CLUB...

...AND THERE'S **THE SHELVES** WITH, LIKE, **EVERY** BOOK YOU COULD EVER WANT.

I MEAN...

...**EVERYONE** KNOWS THIS PLACE. IT'S BEEN HERE **FOREVER**.

. . .

. . .

...HOW LONG IS FOREVER, THO'?

...OH, AND AN IMPORTANT NOTE—

...?

OUR STORE FOLLOWS ADA STANDARDS, AND HAS ACCESSIBLE DESIGN, LIKE NICE WIDE AISLES...

...IN CASE A VISITOR IS ROLLING INSTEAD OF STROLLING (OR USING SOME OTHER MOBILITY AID).

...AND LAST BUT NOT LEAST, WE HAVE THE STOCK ROOM/OFFICE! SUPERVISED BY VICTOR, THE OFFICE CAT.

I ALREADY FED HIM!

hi, victor.

MRROW MRROW

HE PRETENDS ALL DAY THAT NO ONE FEEDS HIM (LIES).

SORRY, IT'S KIND OF CHAOS BACK THERE.

SHUT

RUNNING A BUSINESS HAS A LOT OF MOVING PARTS.

DOES ANYONE HAVE ANY QUESTIONS SO FAR?

SO HOW MUCH MON—

UM.

HOW DID YOU GET STARTED?

AND WHEN?

OOOH, GOOD QUESTION.

MARIA AND I HAVE ACTUALLY BEEN BUSINESS PARTNERS SINCE MIDDLE SCHOOL!

OUR FIRST JOINT VENTURE WAS A LEMONADE STAND.

WE DID PRETTY GOOD FOR TWELVE-YEAR-OLDS, RIGHT?

WE MADE FOUR DOLLARS...

...BECAUSE WE BROUGHT SALT INSTEAD OF SUGAR...

OW, HARD JUDGE! HA-HA!

WELL, WE DID GOOD WITH THIS STORE!

CAN YOU BELIEVE WE STARTED IT WITH JUST A LITTLE BOOK CART IN COLLEGE?

THE SHELF

GOT A TINY SPOT IN THE COLLEGE COMMONS, FILLED IT WITH PRE-LOVED BOOKS AND STUFF WE LIKED.

...WELL.

BOOKS AND STUFF *I* LIKED.

PREEN PREEN

I AM VERY GOOD AT PICKING WINNERS.

haha

THAT'S NOT A BRAG, THAT'S A FACT.

WHATEVER IT IS—IF THEY LIKE IT, SO WILL OUR CUSTOMERS.

SO THAT'S HOW WE STARTED! SHEP IS GOOD AT ITEM CURATION...

...SO THEY STOCKED THE SHELVES...

...AND I HAVE A GOOD HEAD FOR NUMBERS, SO I HANDLED THAT.

AND THEN...

...AFTER A LOT OF MISTAKES...

...AND HAVING TO LEARN STUFF LIKE...

...P&L, TAXES, MARKET CONDITIONS, FOOT TRAFFIC, ZONING, INSURANCE, DISTRIBUTION...

...WE BUILT OUR LITTLE CART INTO A *STORE*!

IT ONLY TOOK US TWENTY YEARS!

...! 20 YEARS?!!!

HA HA HA

HEE HEE HEE

YES, YES, WE'RE *OLD*!

BE QUIET, CHILDREN!

103

...OKAY, NOW, TIME FOR MORE QUESTIONS. WHO'S NEXT?

...

CAN WE PET VICTOR?!

HOW MUCH MONEY DO YOU—

OOH, ME NEXT!

...!
...?

...TIME, EFFORT, THOUGHT...?

EFFORT AND THOUGHT—I'M DOING ALL THAT...

...BUT TIME...LIKE...

...WHAT ABOUT DEADLINES?

THEY KINDA...ALWAYS MAKE THE TIME RUN OUT...

...SUDDENLY...

IT WAS NICE TO GET MY CARD... ONE WEEK AFTER MY BIRTHDAY!

105

OH HIIIIIIII, ALEX ♥

HI, JOSEPH.

UGH

Tess, no!

OH, HEY, UH...TESS?

...

'SUP, 'CITY!

YOU LIKE MANGA TOO? I DIDN'T KNOW THEY MADE ONE FOR *SKORE*!

YEAH, COOL, HUH?

UUUGH

UUUGH

I REALLY WANT TO START PLAYING *SKORE*— IT LOOKS SO FUN!

...

OH YEAH?!

YOU SHOULD. IT'S AWESOME!

...

...OH!

DID YOU GUYS EVER WRITE TO *SKORE*?

ABOUT THE ART FOR YOUR PROJECT?

CAN YOU USE IT?

GLOOOM

....!

WE DID...

THEY SAID NO.

YOU WERE RIGHT, 'CITY.

THERE'S ALL THAT "COPYRIGHT" AND "REGISTERED TRADEMARK" STUFF, AND "LICENSING FEES" FOR USING IT.

OH NO!

...

THEIR EMAIL WAS ALL LAWYER-Y AND LIKE "LEGAL ACTION" FLAVOR.

heh

SOOOO, WE NEED TO GET A DIFFERENT IDEA.

HA-HA, WE'RE STILL COMING UP WITH AN IDEA TOO!

MAYBE WE SHOULD TEAM UP?!

NO!

...

...OR NOT.

ALL RIGHT, EVERYONE, TIME TO HEAD OUT!

...!

WELL, ANYWAY, UH—

MAYBE YOU CAN GIVE ME SOME TIPS ON PLAYING *SKORE*?

OH, FOR SURE, YEAH!

YOU COMING TO JO'S B-DAY PARTY WITH 'CITY?

...!

...

JO, IS THAT OKAY?! COULD I COME?

I'LL BRING YOU THE BEST GIFT!!

u-uh

o-okay?..

YAY!!

THANK YOU, THANK YOU!

What are you doing?

I'm gonna be your wingwoman!

Run interference between you and Jo so you can just have fun!

...WHY DO I HAVE...TROUBLE BELIEVING THAT?

TOO BAD SO SAD!

MAYBE DO WORK NEXT TI—

POP

¿HAY ALGÚN PROBLEMA?

SHE WROTE CRAPPY LINES FOR ME ON PURPOSE!

AND NOW SHE WON'T CHANGE THEM!

HE REFUSES TO DO ANY WORK!!

. . .

AH. OKAY.

...NEW PARTNER FOR YOU! HE ALSO HAD TROUBLE WITH HIS GROUP.

SO YOU TWO ARE VERY GOOD FIT, I THINK.

WHA...

. . .

...HE'S PARTENERED UP WITH YANIC?!

REMEMBER, THIS IS AN IMPORTANT PRESENTATION! BIG PART OF YOUR MARK.

BUT I DON'T WANT A NEW—

OH, GOOD. SOMEONE TO DO MY WORK FOR ME.

HA!

THIS SHOULD BE *GOOD*.

RRRING

UGH, HOW DO WE *STILL* NOT HAVE A BUSINESS IDEA?!

HEY, WE HAVE *PLENTY* OF IDEAS!

YOU JUST KEEP KNOCKING THEM!

WELL, IT HAS TO BE GOOD ENOUGH TO *WIN*!

I MEAN, YOU *SAW* LAST YEAR'S ENTRIES, RIGHT?

YEAH...

MAYBE THIS YEAR'S WON'T BE AS GOOD...?

TESS

WELL, WE *HAVE* TO PICK ONE. THE CLUB MEETING'S TOMORROW!

YOU GOTTA DECIDE!

I KNOOOW shake shake

TEALE

YOU GOTTA HELP ME!!

....?

HUH? NO, I DON'T.

YANIC DOESN'T WANNA DO ANYTHING! HE DOESN'T CARE IF WE FAIL!

OH NO! KINDA LIKE YOU DIDN'T?

I DON'T WANT TO FAIL!! YOU GOTTA TELL THE TEACHER YOU WANT ME BACK IN YOUR GROUP!

WHAT?! I DON'T WANT YOU BACK!

C'MON, I'LL EVEN SAY THE POOP LINES!

UGH, NO WAY!

IF I GET AN F, YOU'RE GONNA PAY, TEALE!

TAKE THAT BROKEN RECORD TO THE STORE. MAYBE YOU CAN RETURN IT!

HEE HEE HEE

IS HE YOUR **NEMESIS** NOW OR SOMETHING?!

UGH, **NO.** MAYBE LIKE, A GAME-GENERATED NPC WITH ONE LINE.

HA HA!

WHAT ABOUT JOSEPH, IS HE THE NEMESIS?

WE'LL SEE HOW IT GOES. ASK ME AGAIN AFTER HIS PARTY.

R-RING

FRIDAY, ENTREPRENEUR CLUB.

···

···

OKAY, EVERYONE, DOING MORE PRACTICE PITCHES TODAY!

REMEMBER, JUST ONE WEEK LEFT TO DEADLINE!

GUH! ONE WEEK?!!

OKAY, THAT'S IT. WE'RE PICKING ONE NOW!

BUT...

NO!

LOOK, I EVEN NARROWED IT DOWN TO FIVE!

ANY IDEA!! THEY'RE ALL GOOD!! JUST PICK!

AAAAH!! OKAY OKAY THIS ONE...!!!

POINT

....!

OOOH!

YEAH, OKAY.

...WHAT DID I GET.

..."LIFT-ME-UP"—

A POSTCARD/LETTER HAND-DELIVERY SERVICE WITH NICE, UPLIFTING MESSAGES FOR A BAD DAY!

...

WE'LL HAVE, LIKE, POSITIVE AFFIRMATIONS AND STUFF, AND CUTE ILLUSTRATIONS ON CARDS.

WE MIGHT ADD CHOCOLATES TOO.

CLAP CLAP CLAP

OH, WOW, THAT'S AN AMAZING IDEA!!

I WOULD BE A CUSTOMER!

CLAP

...

CLAP

WELL, THAT WENT WELL!

LIBRARY

MX. EDI THOUGHT IT WAS A GREAT IDEA!

...

THEY THINK **EVERYTHING**'S A GREAT IDEA, THOUGH.

HEY, 'CITY, HEY, TESS!

SEE YOU AT JO'S PARTY ON SUNDAY, YEAH?

...

OH, WE'LL BE THERE! ♥

...THEY DIDN'T PITCH TODAY. DID THEY NOT COME UP WITH A NEW IDEA?

CHAPTER 5

SATURDAY, TEALE RESIDENCE.

...AND HERE ARE THE TOP TEN AGAIN, FOR THE SEVENTH ANNUAL "PITCH THE FUTURE" —

WE MADE AN ANTI-BULLYING APP! PREVENTION, VICTIM SUPPORT

HI MOM

BUILT A SOLAR-POWERED PROTOTYPE, TO DELIVER TO THE ISS —

— A LUNCH-BUDDY DIGITAL CONNECT SITE! SO THAT KIDS NEVER HAVE TO EAT

AREN'T THESE ALL AMAZING?

CAN YOU BELIEVE THESE ARE ALL JUST TEN- TO THIRTEEN- YEAR-OLD —

CLOSE

...

ALSO! DISTRIBUTION PLANS? THAT'S JUST YOU AND ME, THO'.

DO WE JUST WRITE THAT...?

WE ALSO HAVE TO FILM THE PITCH VIDEO.

ARGH! WE HAVE LESS THAN A WEEK! HOW ARE WE GONNA DO ALL THAT?

UHHH, THE USUAL WAY?

LAST-MINUTE DEADLINE PANIC?

WHAT SHOULD WE DO FIRST— THE PROTOTYPE?

HOW DO WE PRINT—

....!

FELICITY, WHY ARE YOU STILL IN BED?

HUH?

HUSTLE! WE HAVE TO DO YOUR HAIR! WE'RE LEAVING AT ONE!

WHAT?

LEAVING WHERE?

LETTY'S PIANO RECITAL!

THAT'S THIS WEEKEND?

YES!

DID YOU FORGET?

119

SHE HAS SO MANY!!

IT'S CONSTANTLY SOME COMPETITION OR AWARD OR RECITAL OR WHATEVER!

DO I HAVE TO GO TO ALL OF THEM?!

YES!!

...YOU WANT TO SUPPORT YOUR SISTER, RIGHT?

. . .

UH.

THERE IS ONLY ONE RIGHT ANSWER TO THIS QUESTION.

HI, GRAMMIE, HI, GRANDPA!

MY GOODNESS, LOOK AT YOU TWO BEAUTIFUL BLOSSOMS!

SHE DOESN'T NEED SUPPORT. SHE'S NOT EVEN NERVOUS!

EVEN THOUGH SHE'S GONNA BE ON STAGE IN FRONT OF ALL THESE PEOPLE...

HER SELF-ESTEEM IS LIKE...TEN FEET TALL, THREE HUNDRED POUNDS OF MUSCLE, AND WEARS **SHADES.**

'SUP, MORTALS

LETTY'S CONFI-DENCE

WHY WOULDN'T IT BE.

SHE'S NEVER FAILED AT ANYTHING.

CLAP CLAP CLAP

MUST FEEL NICE...

...AND WHAT ABOUT YOU, JELLY BEAN?

....!

WHA—?

HOW IS THAT BUSINESS THING GOING?

ANYTHING WE CAN BUY YET?

I GOT MY WHOLE CHURCH GROUP ON STANDBY. WE'RE WAITING!

O-OH, UH, WE'RE UM...

WORKING ON A PROTOTYPE NOW. AND, UM, DISTRIBUTION...? PLANS...?

OH WOW, PROTOTYPE! DISTRIBUTION! SERIOUS TALK!

OH, JOAN, YOU GOTTA HEAR THIS, THEY GOT A GREAT IDEA.

TELL THEM YOUR IDEA, BABY!

O-OH, UM.

W-WE, WE'RE DOING A, A POSTCARD/LETTER HAND-DELIVERY SERVICE WITH, LIKE, NICE UPLIFTING MESSAGES FOR A BAD DAY?

WITH OUR ART AND STUFF...

IT'S CALLED "LIFT-ME-UP."

...WE MIGHT ADD CHOCOLATES...?

OOOOOOH

JELLY BEAN, THAT'S SO GOOD!

OH, MY GIRLS IN THE GROUP *ALWAYS* NEEDING POSTCARDS TO SEND!

AND HAVING BAD DAYS!

RIGHT? I GOT PEOPLE AT WORK WANTING IN TOO.

YOU'RE GONNA HAVE *DEMAND*, JELLY BEAN!

...REALLY?

...YOU'RE STILL DOING THE PROTOTYPE...? WHAT ABOUT THE BUSINESS PLAN AND STUFF?

....!

DEADLINE'S THURSDAY. YOU GONNA FINISH ON TIME?

...

YES, I AM. THANK YOU FOR YOUR CONCERN.

I'VE GOT THE WHOLE SUNDAY TOMORROW, AND—

BABY, YOU HAVE JOSEPH'S B-DAY PARTY TOMORROW. AT ONE?

!

OH YEAH.

SUNDAY, JO'S HOUSE.

THANK YOU FOR THE RIDE, MR. TEALE!

NO PROB! STAY OUT OF TROUBLE!

OKAY, LET'S GET THIS OVER WITH QUICK, THEN GO BACK TO WORK ON THE BUSINESS PLAN.

UH, YEAH, YEAH, FOR SURE!

HIIII, ALEX!!

OH! HEY...! UH...YOU?

I NEED THOSE TIPS ON PLAYING SKORE!

JUST A QUICK VISIT, RIGHT, TESS?!

RIGHT...?

I HAVE A BAD FEELING ABOUT THIS.

HA HA HA CHASE CHASE HA HA

YAMMER

HA HA HA HA

NO, NO, TO THE LEFT, THEN A BUTT CIRCLE.

WHAT? HOW?

THIS DANCE IS SO STUPID!

AND THIS IS WHERE YOU CHECK SUPPLIES.

OOOH, I SEE.

UH.

HAPPY BIRTHDAY.

. . .

THANKS.

OKAY, EVERYONE, FOOD IS OUT. COME HELP YOURSELVES!

FOOOOOD

OH WOW, IS THAT SUSHI?

NO, IT'S GIMBAP. IT'S KOREAN.

SUSHI'S JAPANESE.

OH.

SCARF SNARF

MRS. KOH'S GIMBAP IS THE BEST. YOU HAVE TO TRY THE GALBI TOO, AND THE SKEWERS, AND THE—

ARGH. I'D FORGOTTEN HOW GOOD MRS. KOH'S FOOD IS...

OM NOM NOM

I USED TO...HAVE IT A LOT MORE.

...

...!

THAT'S ME! FROM THAT...

...PAJAMA SLEEPOVER PARTY WE DID... LIKE FOUR YEARS AGO?

DIDN'T KNOW THEY HAD THAT ON DISPLAY.

JO PROBABLY HATES IT...

...UGH. SHE'S STILL AT IT.

HEEEY, 'CITY.

....!

UH, HEY.

WHY YOU OUT HERE?

YOU OKAY?

UH, YEAH. JUST...

WANTED SOME QUIET.

haha

YOU AND JO ARE LIKE CLONES OR SOMETHING.

?

HE DOES THIS TOO. I DON'T GET IT.

....!

HE'LL, LIKE, EAT LUNCH IN THE LIBRARY TO ESCAPE FUN.

...IS THAT WHY HE WAS IN THE LIBRARY THAT TIME...?

...

SO, UH.

WHAT'S THE DEAL WITH YOU TWO ANYWAY?

IT GETS, LIKE, SUPER-AWKWARD LATELY...

UGH, I DON'T KNOW...

HE JUST GETS ALL WEIRD.

SO DO *YOU!*

haha

I MEAN, UH.

YEAH, OF COURSE. I GOT YOUR BACK...

FOR REAL?!

OMG THANK YOU THANK YOU THANK YOOOU

YOU'RE AMAZING!

U-UH, THANKS!

...

Y-YOU'RE PRETTY COOL TOO...

HA HA

MAN, IF YOU CAN FIND IT OUT...!

I MEAN, I DON'T EVEN CARE WHAT IT IS ANYMORE.

I JUST NEED TO KNOW.

HA-HA, I BET. I WOULD TOO.

...CAN YOU ASK HIM TODAY...?

UH...

I'LL TRY?

NO PROMISES.

BZZ

HUH?

...OOP, IT'S MY DAD.

HE'S COMING TO PICK ME UP.

...I BETTER GO FIND TESS.

TEXT ME IF YOU FIND OUT ANYTHING FROM JO!

UH, YEAH, YOU GOT IT!

LATER!

PEEK

?

knock knock

TESS, ARE YOU IN THE BATHROOM?!

YOU OKAY?

NO TESS! PRIVACY PLEASE!

ACK

S-SORRY MR. KOH!!

WHERE IS SHE?

...TESS?

OH, SHE JUST LEFT. HER MOTHER PICKED HER UP.

LEFT?! WHA...

YES, SUDDEN STOMACHACHE, I THINK!

HUH, SHE DIDN'T EVEN TEXT ME...

I GUESS HER MOM GOT HERE QUICK.

TYPE TYPE

HEY, U GONNA B OK?

IT'S TOO BAD. I WAS JUST PUTTING OUT MORE DESSERT...

MORE OF WHAT NOW?

THOUGH I THINK EVERYONE'S KIND OF FULL.

ZOOM

THE WEAK ARE FULL.

THE STRONG GET MORE DESSERT!

TIP TOE

BETTER BE QUICK BEFORE DAD GETS HE—

SO, UH, ANYWAY...

WHAT'S THE DEAL WITH YOU AND FELICITY?

YOU'RE KINDA...COLD TO HER?

I THOUGHT Y'ALL WERE FRIENDS.

....!

...

C'MON, TELL! IS IT SOMETHING Y'ALL CAN WORK OUT?

IT'S BEEN REEEEAL AWKWARD FOR EVERYONE WHEN WE GAME.

DIVE

...

... IT'S...

...SHE TALKS TOO MUCH.

WHAAAAT! SHE TALKS LESS THAN *ME*! YOU THINK I TALK TOO MUCH?

WHA—? NO, THAT'S NOT...

SHE, SHE TELLS PEOPLE STUFF ABOUT ME. LIKE, MY *LIFE*?

....!

WHAT?!

NO, I DON'T!

GUH

....!

WERE YOU SPYING?!

NO!

I WAS GETTING **DESSERT!**

AND THEN **YOU** BARGED IN!

....!

IT'S **MY** HOUSE!

WHAT DO YOU **MEAN** I SAY STUFF ABOUT YOU?

I **DON'T!**

...Y-YES YOU **DO!**

Y-YOU...

YOU TOLD THEM ALL SORTS OF STUFF! LIKE...WHAT I LIKE, WHAT GAMES I PLAY, WHAT SHOWS I WATCH!

....!

BECAUSE... BECAUSE I WAS TRYING TO INTRODUCE YOU TO THE GROUP!

JUST SAYING THAT YOU'RE COOL!

YOU TOLD THEM ABOUT ELEMENTARY SCHOOL STUFF!

EVERYONE WENT THERE!

IT'S **RELATABLE CONTENT!!** AND WE WERE **COOL** IN ELEMENTARY, SO IT'S REALLY—

... ...I-I...

...WAS THAT A SECRET?

I DIDN'T... ...I MEAN, *EVERYONE* BACK THEN KNEW!

...WAS IT? A SECRET?

...

I'M *SORRY.*

I DIDN'T... I WAS JUST TRYING TO HELP.

Y-YEAH, MAN! SHE WAS JUST TRYING TO HELP!

...

YOU MAD AT HER *HELPING?*

THAT'S...

THAT'S NOT THE *POINT!*

IT...IT'S *MY* LIFE!

...WHY DO *YOU* GET TO TELL IT?

TO...

TO *EVERYONE?*

I-I...

I WAS JUST...

TRYING TO BE A GOOD FRIEND.

OH, THERE YOU ARE!

FELICITY, YOUR DAD IS WAITING FOR YOU OUTSIDE!

THANK YOU, MRS. KOH.

FOR EVERYTHING. GOOD-BYE.

....!

IS... EVERYTHING ALL RIGHT?

...JOSEPH?

...

...DID SOMETHING HAPPEN?

WELL, THAT SETTLES IT.

KTK

HE DOES HATE ME.

SO...

I GUESS...

...IT'S OFFICIAL...

NAME:
   Joseph Koh
STATUS:
   friend??

not anymore

KTK

BUCKLE UP, WE GOTTA GET TO THE STORE AND—

WHERE'S TESS?

...UH.

SWEET PEA, YOU ALL RIGHT?

CHAPTER 6

MONDAY.

RRRING

YOU KNOW HOW THEY SAY, "SLEEP ON IT, AND THINGS WILL SEEM BETTER IN THE MORNING?"

SLAM

WELL, I DID THAT. AND THINGS STILL SUCK.

TESS HAS BEEN IGNORING MY TEXTS SINCE YESTERDAY.

AND WAS ALL WEIRD IN HOMEROOM.

NO IDEA WHAT'S GOING ON.

RRRING

GLARE

SPANISH.

WE'RE SUPPOSED TO WORK ON THE PITCH DURING LUNCH...IS SHE EVEN GOING TO SHOW UP?

IN SPANISH, THERE'S STILL THE DENNIS PROBLEM.

141

THIS JELLYBRAIN'S BEEN TRYING TO HARASS ME, BUT LIKE...

it's for u. pick it up. ...

PLOP

...WITH F-GRADE ABILITY...?

HMM, ¿QUÉ ES ESTO?

IGNORE

HMM. THIS IS PRETTY RUDE.

WHOSE HANDWRITING IS THIS?

LOOKS FAMILIAR...

I CAN MATCH AND FIND OUT.

REMINDER TO ALL— BULLYING AND HARASSMENT IS WRONG! ALSO, GROUNDS FOR EXPULSION.

RRING

UGH, I GOT BIGGER STUFF TO WORRY ABOUT. THE COMPETITION, TESS, AND—

THE OBVIOUS.

HA HA HA
it was awesome.
haha thanks.

· · ·

...I WONDER WHAT HE TOLD THEM... ABOUT ME...

I DON'T WANT TO FIND OUT.

'CITY! WAIT!

HEY, YO, YOU ALL RIGHT?

· · ·

PFFT. YEAH.

I'M FINE.

OH, OKAY.

GOOD...

UM, ABOUT, THE SKORE TOURNEY THIS SATURDAY, I WAS THINKING—

UM, I DON'T THINK I'M GONNA GO.

...HUH?

IT'S JUST... GONNA MESS UP EVERYONE'S FUN.

YOU SAID IT TOO... IT'S WEIRD WITH ME AND JO.

SO I'M JUST... NOT GONNA PLAY CO-OP FOR A WHILE.

...OH. UH.

...

WELL, GUESS I'LL SEE YOU, UH...

ENTREPRENEUR CLUB? ON FRI—

OH! WAIT, NO.

WE'RE NOT DOING THAT ANYMORE.

...!

YOU'RE NOT...DOING THE CONTEST?

UH, NAW, WE KINDA WEREN'T FEELING IT ANYMORE.

SHRUG

SO WE JUST BENCHED THE WHOLE THING.

RRRRRING

OH.

OOP, THAT'S CLASS.

...UH.

HEY, WAIT. UM.

WHAT?

...

...

UM, NEVER MIND.

okaaay. WELL, I GOTTA GO!

SEE YOU LATER!

YEAH, YEAH! LATER!

WHY'S HE BEING ALL WEIRD SUDDENLY?

LUNCH.

...SPEAKING OF WEIRD...

UH, HEY.

...

HEY.

...WELL, AT LEAST SHE DID SHOW UP...?

...ALEX AND JOSEPH ARE DROPPING OUT OF THE CONTEST.

THEY WON'T DO THE CLUB ANYMORE.

...WHA—? WHY?

UH, THEY WEREN'T "FEELING IT"?

...OH.

...

WELL, WHATEVER.

LESS COMPETITION, I GUESS...

. . .

...OKAY, WHAT'S YOUR DEAL? YOU'VE BEEN *WEIRD* EVER SINCE JO'S PARTY!

WHAT'S THE PROBLEM?

NOTHING!

IT'S *NOT* NOTHING!

YOU JUST DITCHED ME! YOU GHOSTED! I THOUGHT YOU WERE IN THE HOSPITAL OR SOMETHING!

WHAT'S YOUR PROBLEM?!

...I... I!

I REALLY LIKE ALEX AND I THINK HE LIKES YOU!!

AND I'M REALLY JEALOUS!!

what.

UGH, I'M TRYING TO DEAL WITH IT, BUT IT'S HARD.

SO...YOU *DO* LIKE ALEX?

BUT YOU SAID, BEFORE—

OKAY, UH...

...BUT... YOU THINK... HE LIKES... ME?

...YES. UGH, HAVE YOU SERIOUSLY NOT NOTICED?!

I LIED! I REALLY LIKE HIM!

ARE YOU *SURE*?!

I MEAN, HE'S SUPER-FRIENDLY TO EVERYONE...

HE TURNED ALL RED JUST TALKING TO YOU ALONE!

ARGH!!

I'M SO JEALOUS.

I WANT HIM TO LIKE ME!

HUH.

uuugh

...ANYWAY.

THAT'S MY PROBLEM.

I'LL GET OVER IT.

SORRY FOR DITCHING YOU AT THE PARTY.

147

SLAM

SO...ALEX...

...MAYBE LIKES ME?

...AND JOSEPH HATES ME...

GLAD I BAILED ON SATURDAY'S TOURNEY! THAT WOULD'VE BEEN AAAAWKWARD...

...

SHOULD I GO AND SAY H—

. . . . !

BICKER BICKER FIGHT

ARGH, YOU'RE SUCH A PAIN!!!

YOU'RE THE PAIN!!

WE HAVEN'T EVEN TOUCHED THE BUSINESS PLAN!

SLAM

UUUGH

DING DING

HUH?

...GRANDMA?! I'M IN SCHOOL! WHAT...?

OH, JELLY BEAN, I JUST HAD TO TELL YOU RIGHT AWAY —

I GOT YOU AN INVESTOR!

...!! you what

AN INVESTOR! FOR YOUR CARD BUSINESS!

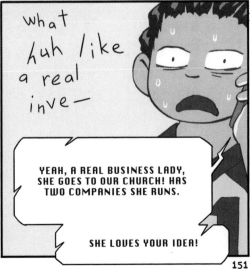

what huh like a real inve—

YEAH, A REAL BUSINESS LADY, SHE GOES TO OUR CHURCH! HAS TWO COMPANIES SHE RUNS.

SHE LOVES YOUR IDEA!

TIC TOC TIC TOC TIC TOC TIC TOC TIC TOC

mission statement?
marketing strategy...
sales projection?
funding?
distribution...
product...
lifecycle...

UUUUGH there's so much... we can't do this... not in two days.

...WE SHOULD GET HELP.

OMG.

WE SHOULD ASK YOUR SISTER!!

SHE'S ALL SCIENCE AND MATH! I BET SHE'D BE GOOD AT THIS!

U-UH WAIT, HANG ON...

...

COME ON, HEAR ME OUT— SHE COULD DO ALL THE *FINANCE* STUFF!

AND WE COULD BE THE ART AND WRITING MUSCLE!!

WE'D BE A **POWERHOUSE!**

WE'D HAVE TO SPLIT THE PRIZE MONEY WITH HER, BUT—

UM...

gloat gloat

HA HA HA

OH, I **SEE.** HAVING TROUBLE **FINISHING A THING? AGAIN?**

I...I MEAN, IT'S NOT TOO LATE TO ADD ANO—

I DON'T WANT TO ASK MY SISTER!!

. . .

W-WE DON'T NEED HELP! WE HAVE BRAINS TOO!

AND...AND **INTERNET!**

WE CAN DO THIS OURSELVES!

RRRING

LAST DAY BEFORE CONTEST DEADLINE.

WE AREN'T EVEN CLOSE TO BEING DONE.

ARGH!!

I KNOW!! DID YOU GET THE CARD PROTOTYPES?

NO, THE FILES WOULDN'T OPEN AT MY DAD'S WORK!

HE'LL TRY PRINTING AGAIN TODAY.

BUT WE HAVE TO DO OUR *VIDEO*!

PFFT, IT'S JUST A ONE-MINUTE THING! WE COULD DO THAT IN HOMEROOM TOMORROW.

FINISHING THE BUSINESS PLAN IS *WAY* MORE IMPOR—

OH! HEEY, 'CITY!

UH.

HEY, ALEX.

HEY, 'CITY'S FRIEND!

MISSING YOU IN *SKORE*, 'CITY! COME BAAACK!

haha

LATERS.

UH, SURE... LATERS.

. . .   ...YOU OKAY?

LUNCH.

MRS. PRATT!!

YEP. I'M **OVER** HIM.

HE CAN'T EVEN REMEMBER MY NAME. pffft

YES?

I'M LOOKING FOR MX. EDI—DO YOU KNOW WHERE THEY ARE?

MX. EDI?

I BELIEVE THEY ARE AWAY WITH A FAMILY MATTER TODAY.

THEY WILL BE BACK TOMORROW MORNING, MAYBE?

...OH.

I KNOW THEY NEED TO SUBMIT THE CONTEST ENTRIES BY NOON.

UH, OKAY, BAD NEWS— MX. EDI ISN'T IN TODAY.

WHAT?! BUT...!!

YOU SAID THEY CAN HELP US WITH THE BUSINESS PLAN!

WELL, THEY AREN'T HERE!

BUT WE *NEED HELP!*

...WE NEED TO ASK YOUR SISTER.

NO.

...DO YOU WANT *ME* TO ASK HER?

NO!! ARGH.

WE CAN DO THIS *OURSELVES!!*

L-LOOK— I WROTE OUR MISSION STATEMENT!

UM.

TWO VERSIONS— FIRST IS "THE FUTURE IS KIND."

THE SECOND IS "A KINDER FUTURE IS IN THE CARDS"?

...I WAS TRYING TO... TIE IN THAT WHOLE "PITCH THE FUTURE" BIT, KINDA?

I LOVE THAT!

I LOVE THEM BOTH!!

YOU DON'T THINK THEY'RE KINDA...CHEESY?

THEY ARE, I LOVE THAT!

ARGH NO! NO CHEESE!!

I-I MEAN THEY AREN'T!! THEY ARE SUPER-COOL. WE SHOULD USE THEM. GIVE THEM HERE.

157

UUUGH

...DID YOU DO THE MARKETING/DISTRIBUTION IDEAS LIST?

YES, I DID! TEXTING NOW. PRETTY PROUD OF THESE.

scroll scroll

...ARE YOU FOR REAL WITH THESE?

...?

...CARRIER PIGEONS...TRAINED DELIVERY CATS...?!

...SKYWRITING?!

WHAAAT! IT'LL MAKE OUR PITCH STAND OUT!

BUT THESE ARE *RIDICULOUS*!!

NO, THEY'RE OUT-OF-THE-BOX THINKING!

CONTESTS *LOVE* OUT-OF-THE-BOX STUFF!

BUT... THIS IS...

CARRIER PIGEONS WILL POOP ON PEOPLE'S CARDS! SO WILL CATS!

AND DID YOU EVEN LOOK UP HOW MUCH SKYWRITING *COSTS*? THIS IS *STUPID!*

THERE'RE WAYS TO MAKE THINGS WORK!!

WHY DO YOU ALWAYS JUST SHUT DOWN MY IDEAS?!

NONE OF MY IDEAS ARE EVER GOOD ENOUGH FOR YOU!!

WHY DID YOU EVEN ASK ME TO BE YOUR PARTNER?!

BECAUSE THE STUPID ENTRY HAS TO BE BY A TEAM!!

THAT'S...

...THE ONLY REASON?

HUH?

...UH.

AM I JUST...

...A FAKE PARTNER?

TO SUBMIT WITH?

W-WAIT, UH, I DIDN'T MEAN—

...YEAH, YOU DID.

...IT EXPLAINS A *LOT*.

· · ·

U-UH, NO, LOOK, THAT CAME OUT WRONG, I-I...

RRRRING

SLAM

THURSDAY.

...IT JUST...ALL CAME OUT WRONG!

I MEAN...I LOOKED FOR A PARTNER BECAUSE I HAD TO...BUT...

...I ASKED **TESS** OUT OF EVERYONE...BECAUSE I THOUGHT SHE'D BE COOL...

...BUT THEN SHE HAD THOSE **RIDICULOUS** IDEAS!

I MEAN, WHAT—

WAS SHE EXPECTING ME TO LIE? SAY I LIKED THEM?!

THEY WERE **BAD IDEAS!**

UGH

I JUST WANTED SOMEONE WHO'D...

...!

SPLAT

#

...BE RELIABLE...

...AND DO THEIR SHARE OF THE WORK.

WHA...

IT'S THE CARD PROTOTYPES.

DAD PRINTED THEM.

...!

SHE TRIMMED AND FOLDED THEM ALREADY...

... UM.

DO YOU...

...

...WANNA DO THE VIDEO?

...

...

...

SURE. WHATEVER.

SHE DIDN'T SAY A WORD DURING THE WHOLE MINUTE...

...AND THEN LEFT AS SOON AS THE BELL RANG.

...

...BUT I GUESS WE ARE STILL PARTNERS...?

THE FUTURE IS KIND

entrepreneur proposal by

Felicity Teale and Tessa Winston

for PITCH THE FUTURE

LIBRARY

UM, MX. EDI?

AH, FELICITY, THERE YOU ARE!!

GOT THE SUBMISSION ALREADY?

UM, IT'S... NOT TOTALLY COMPLETE.

MISSING A COUPLE SECTIONS...

COULD YOU HELP ME FILL IN SOME THINGS?

I'M SORRY, THERE'S NO MORE TIME LEFT!

WE CAN JUST SUBMIT WHATEVER YOU GOT!

WE'LL KNOW TOMORROW WHO GOT IN!

PITCH THE FUTURE!

TOP PRIZE
$1,000
+ PITCH TO INVESTORS

ANYONE CAN **CHANGE THE WORLD!**
COULD IT BE

YOU?!

CALLING ALL
PROBLEM-SOLVERS, FUTURE LEADERS AND **CHANGE-MAKERS!**

CAN YOU COME UP
WITH AN IDEA THAT WILL
SHAPE THE FUTURE?!
PITCH IT FOR THE **WIN!**

...

YOU STILL DRAWING THAT SILLY ANIMU STUFF?

I EVEN GOT YOU AN INVESTOR!

TOOOLD YA! YOU CAN'T FINISH ANYTHING.

WERE YOU SERIOUSLY EXPECTING TO WIN?

OKAY, FINE, YOU CAN EAT IN THE CAR!

BUT FIRST, YOU TWO ARE GOING TO WISH EACH OTHER *GOOD LUCK.*

FELICITY'S GOT A BIG DAY TODAY TOO!

SHOVE

....!

HOVER

UH.

GOOD LUCK.

YOU CAN DO THE THING.

...

THANKS.

YOU TOO.

SO EXCITED FOR YOU BOTH!!

THANKS, MOM.

...ONLY ONE OF US NEEDS THE GOOD LUCK.

RING

LUNCH.

DO YOU KNOW IF YOU WON YET?!

S-SEE?? IT'S NOT JUST ME!

SO WHAT DO YOU WANT, A MEDAL?!

YOU ALL SUCK AND I HATE YOU!!

...B-BUT...

...WE'RE ALL STILL FRIENDS, RIGHT...?

...

WELCOME BACK, EVERYONE!

EXCITING DAY— I HAVE THE RESULTS OF WHOSE HARD WORK GOT SELECTED FOR THE FIRST ROUND OF "PITCH THE FUTURE."

RRRING

NOW, REMEMBER— YOU ARE *ALL* WINNERS, WHETHER YOU GOT IN OR NOT!

YOU WORKED *HARD* AND DID SOMETHING NO ONE ELSE HAS!

. . .

...SO GIVE YOURSELF A ROUND OF APPLAUSE!

CLAP CLAP CLAP CLAP

UGH, JUST READ THE RESULTS ALREADY!!

TWO TEAMS FROM OUR VERY OWN CLUB GOT SELECTED!

SAFIYA, MARISSA, AND JULES ARE THE FIRST TEAM— WELL DONE!!

CLAP CLAP M

CLAP CLAP

AND THE SECOND TEAM WAS, UM...

IT WAS, UH...

...OH, HERE! SECOND TEAM WAS—

LIBRARY

WE DIDN'T MAKE IT...

WAH...

I REALLY WANTED TO GET IN...

YEAH...

NOT US.

KINDA GUESSED THAT.

BUT...

STILL.

hhuh snff

NOW I HAVE TO...

...TELL EVERYONE.

...OF COURSE, OUR PROJECTIONS **ALWAYS** ACCOUNT FOR THE UNEXPECTED—

· · ·

TIC TOC TIC TOC

LETTY'S STILL NOT BACK FROM HER THING...AND MOM'S IN ALL THE MEETINGS.

IT'S FRIDAY, SO GRAN AND GRAMP WILL COME OVER FOR DINNER...

· · ·

GREAT.

I CAN JUST IMAGINE HOW THAT'S GONNA GO.

JUST WANNA...

...HIDE IN MY ROOM...

...AND NEVER COME OUT AGAIN...

...!

KTK

...THAT'S ACTUALLY A SOLID PLAN.

GONNA DO THAT.

WE'RE HOME!

...

I THINK LETTY'S GONNA NEED ICE CREAM, STAT!

MAYBE I CAN STILL HID—

....?

SNF

175

...YOU DIDN'T GET INTO THE COMPETITION?

...

...NO.

AWW, BABY, I'M SORRY. I KNOW HOW MUCH YOU WANTED IT...

BUT...YOU FEELING OKAY, THOUGH?

...

NO!

I FEEL HORRIBLE!

LETTY WAS RIGHT... I COULDN'T EVEN FINISH IT ON TIME!

I LOST FRIENDS, I MADE ENEMIES—

AND I DIDN'T EVEN WIN ANYTHING!!

I FEEL LIKE... ALL I DO IS FAIL!

. . .

OKAY.

WELL.

FIRST OF ALL— THAT'S NOT TRUE.

SECOND—SO WHAT IF IT WAS?

177

178

MA, DINNER TOMORROW, ALL RIGHT?

NO, NOT TONIGHT.

DAD CANCELED DINNER AND CALLED FOR EMERGENCY FAMILY MOVIE NIGHT.

ICE CREAM, POPCORN, DOUBLE FEATURE — ONE LETTY'S PICK, ONE MINE.

I HONESTLY COULDN'T TELL YOU WHAT THEY WERE.

I ONLY HAD TWO THOUGHTS RUNNING THROUGH MY HEAD ON A LOOP —

"IT'S OKAY TO FAIL" AND...

..."BE YOUR FRIEND."

OH, AND A THIRD —

"TOMORROW'S ANOTHER DAY."

CHAPTER 7

NEXT DAY.

KNOCK KNOCK

FELICITY BABY, DON'T SLEEP THE DAY AWAY!

OKAY, OKAY! I'M UP!

...

BRSH BRSH

...

BE A FRIEND TO YOU

UM.

...HEEY.

...

...FRIEND?

...

TOO WEIRD.

I support me.

I got my back.

YOU'RE DOING OKAY...

...OKAY?

I KNOW HOW HARD YOU'RE TRYING.

INHALE

...

OKAY.

GOOD TALK.

...!

UH, THANKS?

...

WELCOME.

...YOU OKAY?

...

MEH.

PROCESSING.

183

SLIIIDE

...WAS THAT ONE OF YOUR "LIFT-ME-UP" CARDS?

...!

U-UH...

YEAH?

YOU'RE SUCH A GOOD SOUL, BABY.

I HOPE YOU AND TESS KEEP GOING WITH THOSE CARDS. WHAT A GREAT IDEA.

...

I MEAN, THE CONTEST IS OVER, BUT...

...WE DON'T... **NEED** IT.

RIGHT?

SHUFFLE

GRANDMA FOUND THAT INVESTOR PERSON...

LIFT ME UP

by Felicity Teale and Tessa Winston

...

...TESS STILL ISN'T TALKING TO ME.

BE RIGHT THERE!

HEY TESS YOU COMING TO ART CLUB?

WHY, DO U WANT TO TRASH MY IDEAS SOME MORE

ARE YOU STILL ON THAT

HELLO...?

. . .

WHAT AM I SUPPOSED TO DO ABOUT THAT?

HMM

. . .

DAD, UM...

HEARD MY CODE NAME.

WHAT UP.

CAN WE GO TO THE SHELF TODAY?

YEAH, ALL RIGHT.

THE SHELF
BOOKSTORE

FSSS

MEET BACK IN THE MANGA SECTION?

YEAH.

COOL.

...UM, EXCUSE ME... MX. SHEPARD?

?

DO YOU... DO YOU HAVE TIME FOR A QUESTION?

HEEEY, I KNOW YOU! ONE OF EDI'S KIDPRENEURS?

U-UH, YEAH.

HI.

WELCOME BACK, FUTURE CHANGE-MAKER!

HOW'D THAT CONTEST TURN OUT?

O-OH, UM...

...MY TEAM DIDN'T GET IN.

...AH.

BUMMER.

IT KINDA WASN'T A SURPRISE. WE DIDN'T EVEN REALLY FINISH IT...

...AND I HAD THIS *HUGE* FIGHT WITH MY PARTNER...

HUH, DOUBLE BUMMER. PARTNER STUFF IS HARD.

U-UM, *YOU* HAVE A BUSINESS PARTNER!

D-DO YOU HAVE ANY ADVICE?

WHAT DO I DO IF MY PARTNER KEEPS OFFERING **REALLY** BAD IDEAS?

...

HOW BAD ARE THE IDEAS?

SHE WANTS TO TRAIN *DELIVERY CATS*!

...

HA HA HA!

...OKAY, *NOT* WHAT I WAS EXPECTING.

THAT'S PRETTY OUT-OF-THE-BOX.

...I HAVE TO HEAR MORE.

WHAT WAS HER IMPLEMENTATION PLAN?

I ASSUME SHE KNOWS ABOUT ANIMAL PROTECTION LAWS?

...WAS SHE GONNA MAKE LITTLE OUTFITS?!

...

UH.

I DUNNO.

WE NEVER GOT TO ANY OF THAT.

I TOLD HER IT WAS STUPID...

HA HA! *I* LIKE IT.

UNREALISTIC, MAYBE?

BUT FUN. INTERESTING.

HEE-HEE, DELIVERY CATS...

I'D PAY TO SEE THAT.

BUT, LIKE, WHAT AM I SUPPOSED TO DO WITH IDEAS LIKE THAT?

LET'S SEE...

YOU CAN PRETEND YOU DIDN'T HEAR IT...

...GET A THIRD OPINION...

...RAGE-QUIT, DO IT ALL YOURSELF HOW *YOU* LIKE IT...

...BUT FIRST—

DO YOU *LIKE* THIS PARTNER OF YOURS?

YOU WANNA KEEP THEM? OR FIND SOMEONE ELSE?

. . . . !

. . .

UH...

. . .

BECAUSE, LOOK, TEAMWORK STUFF WILL *ALWAYS* BE HARD...

...AND ONLY YOU ALL WILL KNOW WHAT'LL WORK FOR YOUR GROUP.

PSST!!

...FELICITY, YO, COME SEE WHAT I FOUND!

?

IN THE GIFT SECTION!

LOCAL TREASURES

THEY GOT A *CONSIGNMENT* SHELF *FOR LOCAL ARTISTS!*

THESE ARE ALL FROM AROUND HERE!

!

YOU WERE SAYING YOU NEED A DISTRIBUTION PLAN—

!

WHY DON'T YOU PITCH YOUR CARDS *HERE*?

...

Y-YEAH, I COULD—

...

?

...ONLY...

...THEY'RE NOT JUST *MY* CARDS.

I'D HAVE TO PITCH THEM WITH TESS.

...!

...I THOUGHT Y'ALL HAD A FIGHT?

IS THAT GONNA WORK?

...

...YES. WE'RE GONNA NEED TO MAKE A STOP.

PUTT PUTT PUTT

huff huff

HEEEY, PARTNER.

POP

....!

YOU MEAN "FAKE" PARTNER?! I'M NOT TALKING TO YOU!

PERFECT, THEN JUST *LISTEN!!* LIKE, ONE MINUTE!

YOU ARE NOT A FAKE PARTNER! ALL THAT JUST CAME OUT REAL WRONG, OKAY?

...!

LIKE, I GOT A PARTNER BECAUSE I HAD TO, BUT I ASKED YOU SPECIFICALLY BECAUSE—

I KNEW YOU'D BE A *GOOD* ONE! YOU'RE SUPPORTIVE, YOU DO THE WORK...

...

YEAH, BUT YOU THINK ALL MY IDEAS *SUCK.*

SO, ACTUALLY, YOU HAD AN AMAZING IDEA. AND I SHOULD'VE LISTENED—

...I DID?! WHAT WAS IT?

WAS IT THE DELIVERY CATS—

NO, IT WAS NOT THE DELIVERY CATS.

...ALTHOUGH, LIKE, WHAT WAS YOUR PLAN THERE?

WHAT ABOUT ANIMAL CRUELTY LAWS?

WOULD THERE BE, LIKE, A LITTLE UNIFORM?

....!

...

UHHH... I DON'T KNOW, I DIDN'T THINK ABOUT THAT.

...SO WHAT WAS MY GOOD IDEA?

Oh, um...

mumble

You know...

mumble

...WHAT?

mumble HUH?

I DID **NOT** GET A WORD OF THAT.

...ASKING MY SISTER FOR HELP!!

UUGH...

OH!

...YES!

THAT'S *RIGHT!*

SHE'D BE PERFECT TO HELP WITH THE FINANCE STUFF!

YES...

YES, SHE WOULD BE.

ugh

...WANT ME TO ASK HER?

...

N-NO, I'LL DO IT.

S-SO, UH...

...PARTNERS?

AGAIN?

FUTURE... BOSS PEOPLE?

CHANGE-MAKERS?

YEAH.

...AS LONG AS YOUR SISTER DOES THE ORGANIZING AND FINANCE STUFF.

YES, BECAUSE WE BOTH SUCK WITH THAT.

YES.

AND SO...

...H-HEY, LETTY.

HEY.

SLIIIDE

UM.

NERVOUS ABOUT GRANDMA DINNER TONIGHT?

...!

...NO. WHY SHOULD I BE?

WELL, YOU WERE ALL... "OH NO! FOURTH PLACE! GRANDMA AND THE OTHER SCIENCE NERDS WILL JUDGE ME!"

PFFT I WAS NOT!

YOU TOTALLY WERE.

WELL, MAYBE... ABOUT THE SCIENCE CLUB KIDS, A *LITTLE*. BUT I CAN HANDLE THEM, AND I AM NOT WORRYING ABOUT GRAMMY. SHE LOVES US.

BTW, thanks for the card.

I'm NOT quitting, just FYI.

OH, OH.

GOOD!

GOOD.

HAPPY FOR YOU.

UM.

S-SPEAKING OF THE CARD, UH.

REMEMBER HOW YOU SAID TO LET YOU KNOW IF WE NEEDED ANY HELP?

WELL, WE DO. WE NEED SOMEONE FOR THE MATH AND ORGANIZATIONAL STUFF, AND LIKE, CAN...CAN YOU?!

...HELP?

SURE. YEAH.

OKAY.

...JUST LIKE THAT...?

WHAT.

NO... SNARK? NO GLOATING...?

I MEAN... DO YOU WANT ME TO?

WHO ARE YOU AND WHAT HAVE YOU DONE WITH MY SISTER?!

LOOK, IF YOU MISS THE SNARK, I CAN ADD THAT FOR FREE!

RRING

BERRYBROOK MIDDLE SCHO

...OH!

A NEW TEAM MEMBER! THAT'S GREAT!

GRAB A TABLE!

WHO'S READY TO DO THISSSSSS!!

WOOOO LET'S GOOOO.

YES, much excite very woo

SOOOOOO, I GUESS I SORTED THAT?

FOR NOW, ANYWAY.

EVERYTHING IS BACK TO HOW IT WAS...

ORGANIZED, ACCOMPLISHED

CHAOTIC, MESSY, ALWAYS LAST-MINUTE

...EXCEPT...

...I'M *NOT*...HOW I WAS. NOT REALLY.

EVEN IF THAT MEANS I'LL BASICALLY JUST STUMBLE AROUND A LOT.

. . .

UGH

ARE YOU FIGHTING AGAIN?

STOPPIT! YOU WANNA GET THIS DONE OR NOT?

WHICH I REFUSE TO EVEN FEEL BAD ABOUT BECAUSE, YOU KNOW WHAT?

DEALING WITH LIFE IS A LOT.

DEALING WITH PEOPLE IS A LOT.

IT'S ALL WEIRD AND MAKES NO SENSE.

EXHIBIT #1

. . .

. . .

STATUS: ???? WHO KNOWS.

PLING

THE OTHER DAY—

jokoh_haha liked 28 posts

HE LIKED EVERY SINGLE POST OF MY BIKER ELVES COMIC.

...!

...AND THEN WAS ALL WEIRD ABOUT IT.

RRING

WAIT, WHAT.

...I THOUGHT YOU SAID HE HATES YOU NOW!

THAT'S WHAT I *THOUGHT*!

I MEAN, *WHAT*...?

BUT THEN HE'S, LIKE...

...FOLLOWING ME ON MY SOCIALS...

...LIKING EVERY UPDATE I POST...

...AND DOING THIS WEIRD...IRL HOVERING THING.

THERE HE IS.

DASH

...WHAT IS HE EVEN *DOING*?

i don't get it.

...

...WELL, HE'S SUPER-CUTE— IF YOU GUYS MAKE UP, GET ME A DATE.

WINK

ARGH TESS STAAHP

CAFETERIA

RRRING

SIGH.

COME ON, VENDING MACHINE, GIMME ANSWERS.

OR AT LEAST SOME CHIPS.

POP

...'CITY?

HEEEY!

OOPS, STEALTH FAIL.

...

...OH, UH, H-HEY ALEX!!

IT'S BEEN FOREVER!

WHAT'S UP?!

WHEN YOU COMING BACK TO GAME DAYS?

UH.

UM, WELL... THINGS WITH JO ARE STILL...

...WEIRD? SO I DUNNO.

I DUNNO WHAT'S GOING ON.

HAS HE, LIKE, SAID ANYTHING?

...!

I MEAN... HE LIKED ALL MY COMICS PAGES ON MY SOCIALS.

LIKE, **ALL** OF THEM. SO WEIRD.

OH, YO, HE DID CHECK IT OUT?

NICE.

I TOLD HIM IT WAS AWESOME AND HE SHOULD READ IT.

...

WAIT, WHAT.

...*YOU* LIKE MY COMIC?

YEAH!!

ARE YOU GONNA MAKE MORE? I'VE BEEN *WAITING*!

THE MAIN ELF BIKER DUDE'S MY FAVE—

I LIKE HIS ROAD SPIKES MAGIC!

THAT'S...

...COOL...

AND LIKE, HE'S *COOL* BUT DOESN'T TAKE IT SERIOUS, YOU KNOW?

OH, AND—

IN-DEPTH WORLD LORE KNOWLEDGE

NUANCED STORY COMPREHEN-SION

UH...

ARGH!!

SEE?! HE JUST DID IT AGAIN!

...WHAT?

HE JUST SENT ME SUPPLIES IN *SKORE*!

HE *NEVER* DOES THAT!

WHAT GIVES?!

I THOUGHT HE HATES ME NOW.

HAS HE, LIKE, SAID *ANYTHING* TO YOU?

....!

OH.

UH.

WE ACTUALLY... HAVEN'T HUNG OUT MUCH LATELY.

...OH. WHY?

WELL, THAT... WHOLE THING WITH... HIM AND YOU...

I WAS JUST...

...LIKE, IS THAT HOW HE ROLLS?

WITH FRIENDS?

JUST... DROP THEM BECAUSE...

...THEY MESSED UP ONE THING?

I MEAN, I'M FRIENDS WITH HIM TOO...

CAN YOU...

...PROMISE TO TELL ME IF SOMETHING'S NOT RIGHT?

NEXT TIME?

AND NOT JUST...

...?

...CUT ME OUT?

IT REALLY HURT...

NOT KNOWING.

...

UM...

Y-YEAH. SURE.

AND, AND I PROMISE TO NOT TELL YOUR STUFF...

...WITHOUT ASKING.

O-OKAY.

...TWIST MY RUBBER ARM.

PLEASE EAT UP. THERE'S LOTS MORE.

DON'T MIND IF I DO, THANK YOU!

IT'S SO GOOD TO CATCH UP WITH YOU! IT'S BEEN TOO LONG!

SO, GUESS WHAT, I MISSED SOME STUFF.

...WAIT, YOU PLAY GUITAR NOW?

TRYING, YEAH...

WROTE A COUPLE OF SONGS.

KINDA COLLABORATING WITH, UH...

...

GOTTA SHOW YOU SOMETHING.

BUT YOU CAN'T TELL **ANYONE.**

212

RECOGNIZE HER...?

I JUST RANDOMLY SAW ONE OF HER VIDEOS, AND...

WAAAIT.

IS THAT...

...OLESYA?! THE ONE WHO MOVED AWAY?! YOU FOUND HER??

THIS ALASKAN LIFE

SUBSCRIBE

YEAH, SHE'S GOT HER OWN CHANNEL NOW.

WOW, THAT'S A LOT OF SUBSCRIBERS.

...

...SHE SURE TYPES YOU A LOT OF HEARTS.

...

*...I MISSED SOME **BIG** STUFF.*

*THEY'VE BEEN TALKING FOR **MONTHS** NOW.*

(...THAT'S WHY HE'S BEEN SNEAKING LUNCH IN THE LIBRARY— TO TALK TO HER.)

NO ONE HAS ANY IDEA.

(EXCEPT FOR ME).

!!

HA HA HA HA

...DID Y'ALL STOP FIGHTING?!

ARE YOU ALL GOOD?!

YEP!

FOR NOW, ANYWAY.

YESSSS

FINALLY!!

GAME DAY AT MY PLACE ON SATURDAY!!

BE THERE, BOTH OF YOU!!

OR I'LL KICK YOUR BUTTS!!

YEAH, YEAH, WE'LL BE THERE!

...!

DO YOU...

...LIKE HIM?

!

I DON'T KNOW WHAT U R TALKING ABOUT

...SO...YES, THEN.

SINCE WHEN?!

HA HA HA

...YEAH, I GUESS JO MISSED SOME STUFF TOO.

YEAH, YOU *FINISHED* THAT PAGE. THAT'S *RIGHT*.

BUMP

IT WAS FINAL-BOSS-HARD AND TOOK FOREVER AND YOU *DID IT*.

C'MON, SIS, LET'S GO! GONNA BE LATE!!

IT'S <u>FINE</u>, I'LL BE RIGHT THERE!

...BECAUSE FOR A LOT OF STUFF...

...THAT SEEMS TO BE WHAT IT NEEDS.

AND LIKE, A WHOLE BUNCH OF TRIES.

THE SHELF
BOOKSTORE

SLAM

OKAY, EVERYONE READY?! GOT EVERYTHING?

217

THE END.

Svetlana Chmakova was born and raised in Russia until the age of sixteen, when her family immigrated to Canada. After receiving a Classical Animation diploma from Sheridan College, she quickly made a name for herself with graphic novels such as the award-winning urban fantasy *Nightschool: The Weirn Books* and the manga adaptation of *Witch & Wizard* by James Patterson. Her acclaimed Berrybrook Middle School series, which has been nominated for multiple Eisner Awards, has captivated readers of all ages since the publication of its first volume, *Awkward*, in 2015 and has made her one of the most renown creators in the world of middle grade graphic novels. In 2020, she revisited her beloved world of *Nightschool*, populating it with a whole new cast of characters for younger audiences with the first installment of her new series, *The Weirn Books: Be Wary of the Silent Woods*.

☆ THANK YOU! ☆

to my mom, for always carrying pencils and paper for tiny-tot me in your purse, wherever we went. You kindled an artist and I hope your soul sees me putting that to good use. I miss you so much.

to my dad, for always letting me be what I needed to be and for giving me the space to try things and make mistakes. Thank you for giving me All The Books, art supplies, and for taking me to my first ever comics convention.

to my husband, Patrick, for stoically enduring the chaos of my book production schedules, for holding things together when I couldn't, and for all the hugs when I really needed them.

to JuYoun, for the endless rereads of my messy scripts and for always gently nudging me toward my better work. Thank you thank you thank you, for everything you do.

And a HUGE special thank you to:

Melissa

Effie

Young

Judy

Mya, of Salt and Sage Books

Yen Press Production Team

~Svet! June 5, 2022

GALLERY

PRACTICING TIKTOK DANCES